The Grieving Gift

An Autobiographical Novel

By
Judy Howard

The Grieving Gift- Judy Howard
Copyright © 2018 Judy Howard

For information contact :
Judy Howard at jhoward1935@gmail.com

Although *The Grieving Gift* is based on reality, this is a book of fiction. The characters are fictional and whatever events that occur or scenes that I describe are created from my own imagination.
This is a work of fiction. Names, characters, places, and incidents either are the product of the author's imagination or are used fictitiously, and any resemblance to actual persons, living or dead, business establishments, events, or locales is entirely coincidental.

Other Books by Judy Howard
Available On Amazon

The Cat and Ghost Series
Coast To Coast With A Cat And A Ghost
Going Home With A Cat And A Ghost

The Masada Series
Masada's Marine
Masada's Mission

The Feline Fury Series
Activate Lion Mode
Activate Love Mode (Coming Soon)

The Lost And Found Series
The Grieving Gift
Truck Stop

ACKNOWLEDGEMENTS

I began writing this book, in memory of Sandra Brown, my sister and my best friend. When dealing with her death I came to realize I was losing the only person who had shared my childhood, my parents, my coming of age, my successes and my failures. There was no one else like her on this vast earth.

So of course, I must acknowledge her, first and foremost. Without her, my real life story woud not be what it is today.

I am deeply indebted to my Hemet Writng Critique Group, Jim and Vickie Hitt and all its members. You became like family to me as I shared this story. And you all trudged loyally and patiently by my side, sorting through the pages, which sometimes made little sense to you or me.

I also want to thank my beta readers, who make the final read before the story goes to print. Kristi Zeiders, Julie April, Judy Rhinehimer, Terry Kim Schwartz,

Jerry Mercer, and Vicki Andreotti, your excellent feedback was vital to *The Grieving Gift* .

DEDICATION

When I began writing The Grieving Gift, my intention was to write my sister's story. I wanted the world to know her as I did. The woman who was kind, but believed she was never kind enough. The woman who gave her love with dedication, yet felt undeserving to receive the same in return.

In writing what I believed was going to be her story, I discovered that our personal stories do not belong to us. They are never about us.

My sister's story became the story of others. Because really, isn't that who we are when we come to the end of our journey? We become a part of those whose lives we have touched.

To my dearest sister, Sandra Brown, who taught me courage through her fears, and gave me strength through her weakness. Thank you for The Grieving Gift. My life is forever enhanced.

A NOTE FROM THE AUTHOR

Sometimes you just have to believe. Even if there is nothing in the path ahead, no logic, no scientific proof, no explanation. You just have to trust that burning desire in your gut which compels your heart to reach for a way, and then to continue even when there is no way. That, my friend, is what makes **dreams come true.**

Judy Howard

CHAPTER ONE
2015

On a death watch, you get to know someone. It is like a roller coaster ride. And like most rides, it brings us back to the place we began, reminding us of who we were and who we have become.

My sister, Margaret, was determined to die the way she lived. She lay in her queen-size bed and glanced at the custom-designed bedspread which the hospice health aide had draped carelessly over the back of the nearby fainting couch.

"How many times have I asked her to smooth it out? It only takes a couple of sweeps of the hand to straighten out the wrinkles," Margaret said to me. She gave me a pleading look. "Janice, could you?"

"Sure," I said as I smoothed and straightened the spread.

Now, she eyed my jeans and tennis shoes, then studied my short hair while I performed the insignificant chore. "Did you try styling your hair like I showed you?"

How many times had she shown me how to dampen my hair and thread my fingers through it, sweeping it back? "Come over here," she patted the bed.

I leaned down as she reached up and raked her fingers through my hair. "Like this," she said. "Now go look in the mirror." I stood before the mirror and admired the difference. "See how the flowing lines distract from your full face, making it appear thinner?"

Months ago she stood beside me like she did now, picking and fussing, perfecting a casual style. "Yes, it does look good," I'd say, and then grab my signature cowboy hat, laden with colorful travel pins from everyplace I visited on my RV journeys. I'd slap it on top of my head, to prove I was not superficial like her. That seemed so long ago, but six months is not long when you know your time is short. Today, her efforts pulled at my heart. I would always remember her kindness and determination to send me off into the world as a class act like herself.

My attitude toward our differences had softened. And Margaret also had begun to see me as more than her little sister. "Are you ready to have a best seller?" She asked once as she helped edit my latest book.

I turned from the mirror, leaving the hat resting on the vanity. I smiled and kissed her. "Thanks, I love it." I paused for what I hoped was an unnoticeable moment and tried to memorize her sweet caring attention.

Margaret sank into the depths of her pillow and closed her eyes as I moved about the room, folding laundry and putting it away.

"Opening my eyes takes me away from the sweet spot where I like to live these days," she said.

She did not have to open them to see the majestic nude painting spanning the wall above her headboard. Margaret might be thinner, but,like the piece of art, her own body stretched across the silk sheets with the grace of a peacock's feather. I imagined the painting was a portrait of her, although in all these years no one in her circles had ever said it was, and I knew her family and friends well enough, that no one ever would ask who the portrait portrayed. Margaret tired easily. As she waited for the arrival of her two sons and their spouses to show up for this special meeting she had arranged, she dozed on and off until the doorbell rang. "Can you tell them to come on into the bedroom?"

The two boys' kisses brushed briefly against their mom's cheek as they stiffly hugged their mother. "You'll find a folder on my desk by the printer," Margaret said. "Do you see it there?" She pointed to the file. "It has copies of my financial statements as they stand right now, my will, and a list of my assets. Have a seat. I want you boys to look it over."

The two sons perched on the low fainting couch, their knees almost touching their chests. Michael and Daniel, their thick, auburn hair curling tight against their heads, were not twins, but as adults I had trouble telling them apart.

Michael, the youngest and stockiest, sported a red shadow-beard so popular these days, yet it failed to hide his round, baby-face features. He rose and stepped around his sister-in-law,Denise. Her shining black hair reached down the straight line of her back as she sat in one of two folding chairs. She clasped her hands in her lap. The only movement, was her one thumb rubbing her knuckled fist. She reminded me of an Oriental Barbie.

The muffled chatter of Michael's two year old drifted through the open bedroom window. Michael glanced outside. His wife, Tonya, followed their toddler, who marched around the immaculately landscaped back yard which Michael had designed and charged his mother what he felt was a reasonable landscaper's fee. He approached the desk and, picking up the folder, he opened it. He removed the three copies. Keeping one, he handed one to his brother and sister-in-law, Daniel and Denise, and the third to Margaret.

Margaret raised her chin a little higher as she reviewed the report of her estate. Although all her L.A. friends would consider the estate's value modest, she swelled with pride. This was her gift to her boys. "I want you to go over each item." She said. "You're co-executors. Everything is to be divided fifty-fifty."

As Michael, Daniel and Denise reviewed the papers, Margaret continued, her voice frail. She smiled at me but addressed her comments to her boys. "I don't want you two to have any conflicts, so today I want you to walk through the house and decide if there is anything that may be particularly sentimental to you." Margaret paused as if the speech tired her, but then glanced at me again, as if for reassurance? Or, was she checking for my reaction because I was not named as an heir? I had not expected to be, but wondered if she knew that. "When our mother died, Janice and I were able to go through all the things, dividing them up without a problem." She smiled at me again. "I want to work things out now with you boys, while I'm here to settle your arguments."

The boys looked at each other, each hesitating to go first.

"I would like the bedroom furniture," Michael said.

"Of course, dear. I want you to have it. You put a lot of hours into each piece. It has meant so much to me. You should have it."

Daniel laughed, although to me it always came out as a sneer. "But what's it worth?" He said.

The corner of Michael's mouth twitched in response to the joke. and I don't know how it was possible, but Margaret stiffened even more. Margaret and Michael both ignored the joke, which Daniel implied.

Daniel rose, the action accented his leanness, making him appear taller than he was. He stepped over to his Barbie wife, Denise sitting in the chair at the foot of the bed. Towering over his wife,Denise, he pointed to an item on the list. The couple whispered to one another and snickered.

Margaret zeroed in on her oldest son and daughter-in-law. "What is it?" she asked, "What's the problem?" She struggled to scoot up higher. I rushed to the bedside, plumping up the pillows behind her.

Daniel pointed out the item to Michael, then glanced back at Denise. Denise nodded and said. "It's the value of the Lexus."

"What about it?" Margaret's words rang an octave higher.

Daniel, still grinning, glanced at his brother, then Denise, who sighed and stood. Taking the report, she bent over her mother-in-law and pointed to the entry. "You have the car listed at $8,000.00. The car's fifteen years old. It's no way worth that." The daughter-in-law raised her brows expectantly and stared at Margaret.

Margaret's sunken eyes bore into her daughter-in-law's, but clouded over as if to hold back her irritation. Her lip line twisted.

Denise flinched.

I marveled at Margaret's control. Without losing eye contact, she responded. "You can look up the blue-book value. I'm too tired." The matriarchal remark hit home.

Denise swung around, handing the paper back to her husband, and sat back down. The young woman's narrow index finger pushed a shiny strand of her Asian-black hair away from her temple and tucked the lock behind her ear. "Just saying," she said. "It's no way worth that." She swung her head, flipping her hair from her shoulder and again, folded her hands in her lap.

A spasm flashed across Margaret's face. "As I said, dear, I'm too ill to verify it."

Denise shrank back in her seat. Margaret, again, set her chin at that ever so slightly regal and victorious angle of which was I becoming so aware.

Margaret reminded me of a puppeteer, juggling the family disagreements. It was a good guess she had orchestrated the strings her entire life. And today she proved she hadn't lost her touch. She surprised me that she still had the energy to carry if off.

Her family's aloofness sucked me dry, leaving me itchy and restless wanting to get away. Their values were the reason. During our adult years, I never spent much time with them, and yet, they surprised me. This petty discussion of the Lexus' value was not a class act. What shocked me more is Margaret was not appalled, only irritated her daughter-in-law challenged her appraisal.

This final scene in the bedroom had drained Margaret. Her feather-light body sank deeper into the bed. "I'm going to rest now."

I herded her audience from the room, dimmed the lamp and pulled the shade.

When she awoke, she didn't ask if the boys had followed her instructions. With five o'clock approaching, the boys faced hours fighting the heavy traffic back to L.A. Their applied pecks to their mother's cheek were more relaxed, as well as their hurried half-hugs. Tonya and Denise paraded the grandchildren into the bedroom to deliver their farewells. "Say goodbye to Me Maw." The women followed suit and applied their own quick kisses and then herded the youngsters from the room.

After the last family member exited, I clicked the deadbolt, thankful Margaret's performance, as well as mine was over. We both could rest. Tip-toeing back to the bedroom, I took a deep breath and exhaled. Like drawing the curtain, Margaret smiled at me and closed her eyes, surrendering to the drugs. She drifted away into a thick sleep. I gazed out the bedroom window at the fading day. I, too, longed to run away.

CHAPTER TWO

1954

"He said no." Margaret shut the bedroom door and lowered her voice." Let's do it anyway."

"How?" I whispered because she did. "Dad said no. He said it's going to rain.

Margaret plopped on the edge of my bed and crossed her legs. "We'll run away." The mattress bounced, jostling my library book, *The Black Stallion*, leaning against my folded knees.

I stuck my finger between the pages of my book at the part where the boy, Alec, and the Arabian horse became stranded on the desert island after being shipwrecked. I scooted my back up straighter against the headboard. Margaret always came up with the greatest ideas for adventure. "And how do we do that?"

"We'll have plenty of time after supper. It doesn't get dark 'til nine. I've got it all figured out." Margaret jumped from the bed and moved to her desk. Ripping a page from her lined theme book, she scribbled notes. "Let's see. We'll need a blanket and our pillows. And I'll sneak some bags of chips from the kitchen while they're watching TV." She chewed on the pencil's eraser. "Oh, and a couple bottles of pop."

"How're we going to get all that stuff outside without them seeing? And how're we going to carry it all?" This was the wildest plan she had ever come up with. I might be eight years old but even I knew this was serious stuff.

"You go out after supper and hitch Blackie up to his cart. He loves pulling it and anyway he has to go with us. We can't leave him behind. We've had him since he was a pup. Bring him around to the side of the house and wait right under the attic window. I'll get a rope from the basement and lower everything down to you from the attic window."

Her plan sounded reasonable. Mom and Dad would not catch her up in the attic. They never go up there. "Where're we going to go?"

"We'll camp out at the lake, where we ice skate and go walnut hunting."

"How far is that?' You could not see the lake from the house.

"Not that far." Margaret studied her list and then looked up. "Are you in?" She folded the paper and shoved it in her back pocket. "Don't be a fraidy cat."

It sounded like a real adventure — if we didn't get caught. I loved the woods along the lake. We came across wild creatures, deer, raccoons and sometimes even an opossum. Dad always warned us to keep a lookout for wild pigs and wolves, too, but I'd never seen any. We would have Blackie with us. The eighty-pound lab would protect us.

"I'm in." We both jumped when the door opened and Mom said, "Time to set the table."

The normal limited conversation at dinner felt abnormal because I didn't try to make jokes or be cute like I usually did. Tonight my compulsion to pull Dad out of his ever-brooding mood was tempered by the secret excitement of our plans. Margaret kept her head down, hovered over her dinner plate and ate silently. We rushed through the dishes without our usual bickering.

Margaret's scheme was perfect. Blackie loved the attention, so when I buckled the cart's harness straps, he wagged his tail eager to start the adventure. My heart pounded as Margaret lowered our gear from the attic window. Even a flashlight. Good idea.

We hiked across the road and through old man Davis' pasture. I sang, "Oh, give me a home —" and Margaret chimed in —"Where the buffalo roam."

The sun sank low in the sky by the time we reached the cornfield that butted up against the Davis farm.

The going was easy and soon we had traveled a couple of child miles and could no longer see our home.

Margaret pointed to a grassy patch between the plowed plot of land and the line of barbed wire. Elm trees lined the fence. "Looks like a good place to camp," Margaret said.

The thrill of spending the night outside, under the stars, with no one overseeing us exhilarated me. "Sure, let's stop here." I unharnessed Blackie. Margaret spread the blanket on the ground and plumped the pillows. She set out two bottles of Coke and two bags of potato chips and we sat cross-legged, crunching the snacks and sipping our sodas. I grinned at her. "This is neat! I wonder if we'll get to the lake tomorrow."

"Probably," Margaret said. Her forehead furrowed. "Do you think Mom and Dad are worried about us?"

"What?" I hadn't even thought of them. "I don't know."

"Maybe we should tell them we're running away. You know, so they won't worry."

Leave it to Margaret to think of everything. "I guess so."

"I'll go back and tell them," she said. "You wait here." She grabbed her Coke and traipsed back down the path we had come and disappeared. I stretched back, laying my head on the pillow and crossing my ankles, as Blackie plopped down beside me. Staring up at the trees and watching the fireflies blink in the dimming light, I figured it was probably a good thing that we were telling Mom and Dad. I didn't want them to worry. I dozed off, dreaming of camping on the lake the next night, until Blackie jumped up, wiggling and wagging his tail. Margaret was back.

I sat up. "How did it go? What did they say?" At that moment, I realized it mattered what they had said.

"We have to go home." Margaret picked up her pillow and threw it into the small cart. "Get up. Help me fold the blanket."

"What do you mean, we have to go home?" Blackie looked up at me and nudged my fisted hand.

"We have to go home. Dad said so. He said it's going to rain."

As if the words were a commandment to the universe, raindrops tickled my face.

"Hurry up. Help me fold the blanket."

I stared at Margaret. This trip had all been her idea. Now she didn't have the guts to buck Dad or the rain? Before we had Blackie secured in his harness, huge cold drops pelted us. In minutes, our clothes were soaked.

By the time, we reached the pasture the fallow corn field became a suction machine of mud, pulling at our sneakers and caking the wheels of Blackie's cart. The dog strained against his harness as the thick slime-coated tires bogged down. Stumbling and falling at times, the slick, black paste slid down our pants legs as we pulled ourselves from the mire. The going was slow but I was in no hurry to meet the punishment we most certainly would face.

Tight lipped and rigid, Dad met us on the back porch. "Unhitch Blackie and hose him off. Then go to the basement to clean up."

Whatever Dad felt, he sealed behind his tight, thin lips. I wondered what kept him from shouting. My anger burned in my gut. My own mouth straight-lined not only at Margaret because she ratted us out, but also at Dad strangely for not caring enough to even yell. And yet I followed everyone else's lead, I stuffed it. The next time I run away, I'll do it on my own.

CHAPTER THREE
2015

Margaret patted her thinning hair as she gazed into the mirror and admired the cut and style from my beautician, Candy. "Janice probably hasn't told you, but I've gone to the best hair dressers in L.A." She took the small hand mirror Candy offered and tilted her head side to side to inspect the back of her head. "My hair has never looked as good since I started coming to you, Candy. You're a real treasure." Margaret clutched her hand and slipped a bill into her palm. Her boney fingers folded Candy's around the bill. "This will probably be my last time. I want you to know how grateful I am."

Candy opened her hand and gasped. "A hundred? This is too much." She shook her head. "You don't have to do this." She thrust the gratuity back to Margaret. "It's been a pleasure taking care of you and if you need me to come to the house, I'll be glad to. Just let me know."

Margaret gripped Candy's fingers and pushed them away. "No, you keep it." Margaret squeezed the girl's hand, "It's a shame you couldn't have taken your husband to Cedars Sinai for his surgery. They have the best doctors in the country. I know how difficult it is for you right now, dear."

Candy tried to step away but Margaret still controlled her hand as she lowered her voice and said, "And don't you worry about me, dear. I'm not afraid of dying, but I hate to leave Janice all alone. That's why I moved here, so I could be near her." She patted Candy's hand. "I worry about her, living way out here in Sun City without all the services L.A. has to offer. You know what I mean I'm sure." She raised her brow and gave Candy a knowing nod. "Janice has no one after I'm gone."

"I'm sure she'll be okay." Candy patted Margaret's hand and flashed a weak smile. "Janice says she'll be finishing up her third book soon."

Margaret whispered again to Candy. I'm just glad she's had someone like me with an education to edit her books." She sighed, shaking her head. "But I just couldn't do it anymore."

Candy pulled away, grabbed the broom and busied herself, sweeping up the scant splotches of white hair.

"Ready to go?" I said, picking up Margaret's purse.

"Yes, dear. All ready." Margaret pushed herself up from the chair, cupped Candy's face in her hands and kissed her cheek. "Thank you so much for making me feel beautiful."

After leaving the beauty salon, we made a stop at the bank next. Inching the car into a tight spot near the bank's entrance, I turned to Margaret as I shut off the engine. "Are you sure you're up to going in? I could get the cash for you."

"I'm fine." Margaret gathered up her purse and climbed out.

I hurried around the car and grasped her elbow to steady her. Inside, Margaret nodded toward the furthest teller. "Let's go to Beatrice's window. She's always so helpful."

"I've been coming for over thirty-five years and she was here then." I said as I motioned to the waiting area. "Why don't you sit down and I'll wait in line for you?"

"No, I'm fine."

Beatrice's appearance never changed. Her pageboy hairstyle from the sixties and a thick application of rouge gave the impression she was stuck in her youth and still blushing. "Hello Margaret. You haven't been in for a while. It's so nice to see you. How are you?"

"I'm fine." Margaret handed the teller her withdrawal slip. "I need five hundred in cash. Twenties will be fine."

Gripping the counter, she leaned against it. "I just went on hospice."

"Oh no!" Beatrice paused with her paperwork. "I'm so sorry." Reaching out she rubbed the back of Margaret's hand. "I'm so sorry but you'll be fine. You believe don't you?"

Margaret pulled her hand away. " Actually, I don't." She forced a gracious smile.

"Oh no!" Beatrice eyes grew big, her voice got small. "You don't believe? At all? You do know what will happen if you don't?"

The corner of Margaret's mouth turned down. She couldn't restrain the smirk. " I'm fine."

"But couldn't you just say you believe? You know, just to be safe?"

Margaret's brow furrowed. "And should I say I believe in Buddha, Allah and all the others, just to cover all my bases?"

Beatrice slumped, resting her elbows on the counter. "Oh, no. I guess not." Barely audible, she squinted, laboring over the options, "I see what you mean." She straightened then, her face lit up and she said, "I'll pray for you, Margaret." She seemed cheered with her solution, stood taller and counted out the cash.

Margaret shrugged, gathered up the money, and placed it carefully in her purse. "Thank you, Beatrice."

Back in the car, Margaret collapsed into the seat, closed her eyes and rubbed them. I smiled at her and patted her leg. "Don't you feel better? Beatrice is going to pray for you. Everything is going to be fine." Margaret's voice took on a tone. "And that is why Beatrice has been a teller all her life."

I stared out of the windshield, astonished by my sister's logic. Why had I never noticed her attitude? My sister was much more than a snob, she was an elitist. Before she became ill I would have engaged her in an amusing debate, never realizing her seriousness. Today it struck me, she was adamant.

Margaret blinked at the bright sunshine on the drive home. Exhaustion dug into her bones, setting her eyes deeper in their sockets, yet she held her chin high. I imagined she clung to the small thread of happiness that her hair looked good. At home, she flung her flats off, flopped into bed and crumbled against the pillows. She smiled at me, patting the bedside. "Come sit for a while, before you go?"

I stretched out beside her and said, "Your hair looks good. Candy always does such a nice job."

We stared straight ahead at the TV, watching Andy Griffith and a boyish Ron Howard whistle their merry tune as they ambled down to the Mayberry fishing hole.

Margaret's eyes fixed on her Associates and Masters Degrees on the wall over her dresser. Closing her eyes, she mumbled, "This is not L.A."

"That's for sure. Sun City's not LA, just like Springfield was not Chicago. Remember how you always wanted to go shopping in Chicago?"

She smirked. "Yes, I remember."

"Springfield will always be home, I said. "I'm going to go back and visit all our old haunts — Washington Park, our high school and grade school. Like we did in '87. Remember? "

A weak smile spread across her face. "That visit brought back a lot of memories."

"For sure. Remember our house on Park Ave.? Remember how nice those people who lived there were? They had to work, but they left the door unlocked so we could walk through and reminisce? How nice was that?"

"Pretty stupid if you ask me. We could have robbed them blind."

"Remember how we looked up Dave and Gary?"

Her face softened and she chuckled. "Yes. I should have called Dave, but I didn't want him to think I would have even given him a second thought after all these years."

"Not me! I didn't care what Gary thought. I wanted to know what he was like all grown up. After I got pregnant he was the only person who showed me any kindness. The high school and the entire town had shunned me. My two best friends dropped me like I had the plague instead of a baby. I felt like a piece of trash. Even you. I don't remember you saying anything to me one way or another about what I was going through. Yet, even after getting pregnant by someone else, through it all, Gary still liked me."

Leaning back into the pillows, I drifted away from the sick room and the bleak reality of facing a future without my sister. I floated back to my small basement apartment which I rented from my parents after I had gotten pregnant.

"Gary visited me at the apartment on Fourth Street. He used to hold Charlotte and rock her to sleep. And after I moved to college, he drove the hundred miles to see me there."

"Sure I wanted to call Gary that night. He had been there for me at the most difficult time of my young life. He even asked me to marry him once."

"What did you say?"

I glanced at Margaret and giggled, thinking of the night so long ago at the drive in theater. "Obviously we didn't get married. I didn't take him seriously. told him he was being silly, that he just had too much to drink." I didn't take him seriously. To me our relationship was only about the sex. That was all. Remember when he showed up at our hotel restaurant the morning after I called him?

Magaret nodded.

I gazed out the window, swept up in the memory. "I was so surprised and flustered. Who wouldn't want to meet up with their first love?" My breathing quickened remembering his blue eyes and his secret smile which made me feel it was meant for no one else but me.

I glanced at Margaret. A warmth spread over my face."Was I blushing?" I touched my face.

"Until that morning I saw myself as a forty year old, dowdy married woman. But when he walked in the restaurant? I was sixteen again."

I rose from the bed and began to pace. My memories held me back in that Illinois hotel restaurant. "He was a long haul truck driver. He asked me to write to him. I knew I wouldn't of course, because I was married ––but oh my! It didn't matter to me that he was a truck driver."

"You know the character, Brad, who was the love interest and old high school boyfriend of the main character in my first four books? I created him in the image of Gary."

I pressed my palm to my cheek and jerked my it away, waving it like it had been burned. "Now I'm a sixty-nine year old, dowdy widow woman." I shook my head, unable to believe my reaction after all these years. I spun around, charged with a sexual energy and began fussing with the bed covers. "What is wrong with me? My pulse is pounding, just thinking about him!"

"Did you ever tell Nate you saw him?" Margaret asked.Margaret knew Nate was the jealous sort.

"I did, mainly because of my intense reaction. If I didn't tell, it would have been like hiding something. I told him, "I could sure understand why people had affairs."

"What did he say?"

"I was surprised. He really didn't say anything."

"I was envious that Gary came to see you," Margaret said.

"Really? From all you've told me about Dave, he was pretty hung up on you. If you had called him, I'm sure he would have wanted to see , too. Did you break up with him?"

Margaret hugged her knees against her chest. She raised her chin with that prideful tilt which was becoming so familiar to me. "I did," she said. "He didn't plan to go to college like me. So, I ended the relationship before I moved to Champaign-Urbana." Margaret sighed. "All that was such a long time ago."

"After Nate died, I tried to find Gary, but with such a common last name, I got nowhere."

I stretched and checked my watch. "Gus will be here soon. We better quit talking about old boyfriends. You sure have a good one now."

I gathered up the dirty plate and water glass from the bedside table and carried them to the kitchen. My eyes welled up thinking of how lucky she was to at last have such a warm, mature relationship, during this time of her life. Gus was an unpretentious, quiet and simple man. He treated her with all the love and respect she deserved.

I had dealt with my own jealousy when he came into her life and took up most of her time. I didn't react. He was what she needed. He may not be from L.. but his steadiness and undemanding love was something she had never experienced. She would be able to count on him during the rough days ahead.

I returned to her bedside and sat on the edge. Taking her hand, I said, "When I go back home, I'm going to visit every special place we shared— Lake Springfield where we ice skated in the winter and swam in the summer, and collected bottles out of the trash cans, remember? — The pond at Washington Park where we fished for crawdads and went sledding?—And Sangamon River where Dad took us target shooting— I'm going to visit them all. And I will think of you."

An idea jumped into my head. I squeezed Margaret's hand and sat straighter . "We should make a pact. Right now." Excited by my idea, I tried to restrain from bouncing up and down on the edge of the bed. "I know you don't believe in God or an afterlife."

Margaret shot me a questioning look.

"When you're dead, you're dead," I said. "Isn't that what you think?"

She nodded.

"What if you're wrong?"

What if I am?"

"What if after you're dead you findout that you're wrong? If that happens, I want you to give me a sign."

"A sign? What do you mean?"

I frowned. Thinking out loud,I said, "Oh, I don't know."
 I brightened. "I've got it! Send me A Grieving Gift! Have you ever heard of a Grieving Gift?"

Margaret raised her brow, and grinned. "No, what is a Grieving Gift?"

"A hospice nurse once told me about it. Her grandmother's family believed the deceased would send a grieving gift, a sign if you will, to let a loved one know they were okay. Her grandmother told her of unexplainable events that she believed could only have been at the hand of the deceased loved one.

"I like to call these happenings Grieving Gifts," the nurse's grandmother had told her granddaughter. The "gift," the grandmother said, is someone or something which comes onto the scene after a loved one's death to enrich the lives of those left behind more than they ever could have imagined."

Rolling her eyes, Margaret's mouth turned downward. She smirked, the same expression she used for those she considered beneath her but she tolerated because she liked them.

"Make something incredible happen in my life," I said. "Make me believe you are still watching over me, that you are wrong, that you're not "just dead.""

Margaret would have snorted if the action wasn't so unladylike. I know she believed the conversation silly and tiring. "I don't know what that would be," she said.

"I know! You know how lonely I'm going to be, right?" A deep sadness clouded Margaret's tired features. "Yes, I do," she said. "I told you to start searching for another sister, like Ashley. Isn't that what she is to you now?"

"We're close, but she's not someone whom I would want to burden with the responsibility of caring for me when I'm old. She's a friend, not blood."

My big sister squeezed my hand and kissed the back of it. "I'm sorry. I wish I could change things."

"You and me both," I said and pulled away from the emotional moment. I grinned at her. "I'll be okay," I said.

As I stood my mood brightened and I grinned. "That's it!"

"What?"

"The Grieving Gift! Send me a special person. Someone who loves me and will spend the rest of his life with me."

"A boyfriend?"

"More than a boyfriend. A soulmate." I giggled at my wild imagination. Might as well shoot for the impossible. "And while you're at it make him handsome and charming, too. If that happens, I will know you had a hand in it." The idea took hold and I laughed at my own silliness. "But you have to agree." My late husband, Nate had passed nearly twelve years ago and I had experienced no romantic possibilities, nor had I wanted any, so if what I was proposing did happen, I would definitely call it a Grieving Gift and a miracle.

"And if I am right?" Maggie was enjoying the playful banter.

"If you are right? If you are just dead, finished, done?" I raised my brows. "Well then," I tilted my head and giggled. "I guess I will be alone for the rest of my life and there's no such thing as a Grieving Gift. But you have to agree to try."

Maggie nodded, her lips formed a tight line. "I will. If there is such a thing."

She squeezed my hand and rubbed it gently. My throat tightened. A tear escaped down my cheek. I stared at the TV screen as Andy Griffith and Barney Fife discussed the latest small town crime in Mayberry.

At home that night, triggered by our conversations from the afternoon, I fell into a fitful sleep, dreaming I awoke to the warmth of the cherrywood bedroom walls of my college trailer.

In the dream the room reflected a reddish glow across the sheets and I wondered what Gary was doing in his childhood bedroom at his parents' farmhouse.

What he was doing was what he did every time I thought of him over the years. Everytime my thoughts of him filled me with a heated desire.

Over the years, I dreamed of him often

CHAPTER FOUR
1954

was eight years old. The changing landscape of my mid-western home town, sometimes green, or golden or snowy white, stretched into infinity. My dream was to race bareback on a steed across the open fields, clinging to his muscular neck while his mane brushed against my cheeks and the scent of horse sweat filled my nostrils, just Like the boy, Alec, in my favorite book, The Black Stallion.

I despised chores which tied me down and kept me from exploring the outdoors. Adventure seeking seemed the only way to escape my compulsion to play cheer-me-up to Dad, who struggled with his dark moods.

My ideal weekend began in the kitchen nook around our yellow-marbled-Formica table. Margaret and I gulped down the Cheerios laced milk from our cereal bowls, tossed them into the sudsy dishwater, and raced out the back door.

"Don't slam the ….."

The door banged shut against Mom's words as we reached our Schwinn bikes, leaning against the big elm that shaded the majority of the yard. As if choreographed, our tennis shoes hit the kickstands, planted on the pedals, and standing up for speed, we pumped our way down the long drive like wild horses stampeding from the corral.

"Where do you want to go?" Margaret shouted over her shoulder. A year older, she pedaled stronger and always led the way.

"I don't know. Where do you want to go?" I stood, pushing hard on the pedals to catch up.

"Let's go down the old mine road."

"Okay. Maybe the raspberries are ripe," I said. The old mine road was one of our favorite hangouts. Years of weeds disguised the railroad tracks as a forgotten path, leading to an old mining pit filled with murky water. The place was forbidden.

Dad was a quiet man, so when he said anything, Margaret and I paid attention. "Don't go past the fence that surrounds the pit," he said. "I know you can swim, but I've seen water moccasins." We listened but sometimes intrigue overruled.

I pedaled faster, eager to explore the mysterious area. I loved how Margaret didn't care about the rules. We parked our bikes under the train trestle and hiked, prancing from one rotted railroad tie to the next, making our way down the rusted tracks that used to carry the coal carts from the mine out to the main road.

The morning sun crept higher as we squatted on the banks of the pit watching dragonflies skate across the dark mirrored water. The only sound, plops and splashes from the pebbles we tossed. Ripples crawled across the black water sending the long-legged insects, skimming the surface, to flit up into the heating, humid air.

I pushed up from my squatting position, scoped the surrounding brush and pointed toward the tree line. "Look, Maggie! There's the shaft entrance. The rails keep on going. Do you want to follow them? See how far they go? "

Margaret stood. "I've told you. Don't call me Maggie. We need to go home. We're going out selling today. Remember?"

"Oh yeah, I forgot. I like collecting rags better. It's easier," I sucked on a blade of grass, studying the old railroad tracks, which promised to lead me away to the excitement of new frontiers.

"Let's just go just past the entrance," I said. "Then we'll go back." I scooted down the bank toward a narrow animal trail that led along the fence line.

"Wait up!"Margaret scurried down beside me, but lost her footing, and tumbled against the unstable wire fence. The barrier gave away, the rotted posts collapsed, and the wire netting swung her, sending her splashing deep into the oil-slicked depths.

"Maggie!" I scooted on my butt down to Margaret. Her legs and arms flailed as I reached out to her.

"Don't call me Maggie!"

I rolled back on my heels and sat down among the cattails. "Really, Maggie?" . "You're drowning in a snake infested pond and you're going to worry about me calling you Maggie?"

"I hate you calling me Maggie."

I sprang up. "Eek! Get out of there!" I pointed, shaking my finger. "A snake! It just swam under the fence! Did you see it?" I jumped up and down.

Margaret tried to climb up the bank, flailing her arms even more, but instead she disappeared behind an explosion of water. Reappearing, dripping and drenched, she scrambled up the bank, turned and stared into the depths. "Where? Where is it?"

I screeched, waving my hands. "There!" The moccasin, floated by, threading its way through the cattails. "Let's get out of here!"

We crashed down the unbeaten path to the train trestle and mounted our bikes on the run. Heads down, adrenaline pulsing, we pumped with the force of the locomotives that used to ride the rails until we reached the main road.

Once on the safety of the asphalt pavement, we coasted, leaning back on our bicycle seats and dared to look at each other. Margaret's shirttails, already dry, billowed in the wind. With one hand on the handlebars, she high fived me and we laughed.

"Way to go MAAAGGEEE!" I yelled, laughing even louder. She threw her fist at me, but missed. I taunted again," MAAAGEEE!" And sped off down the road.

"What? Are you chicken?" Margaret glared up at me as I hugged the branch of the cherry tree.

"I've never climbed this high." My arms ached as I clung to the thick tree limb before it veered off in two different directions. One branch stretched up to the sky, while the other reached out, casting its shade across the green grass below.

Margaret cocked her head back and stared up at me. "I dare you to climb higher.". "You're such a chicken. I've been all the way to the top."

"I can't." The bark scratched my arm as I clutched the tree and looked down. "I'm scared. I can't go any farther."

Margaret's taunting only made me tighten my hold on the branch.

"I can't go higher." I began to cry. "I can't."

Margaret shrugged. "Well, stupid, then come on down." She planted her fists on her hips.

I dared to peer down. "I can't. I'm scared."

"Are you serious? You're such a scaredy cat. Come on down." She paced around the tree and glanced at the house. "If I have to call Dad, he's going to be mad." She scratched her head. "Come on. Don't be so stupid."

I cried louder. Margaret would not call Dad. He would blame her for my predicament. She was the oldest, and I was his favorite.

Margaret sucked in her attitude at the sound of the back screen door slamming. Dad strode from the house, disappeared into the garage, and came out with a ladder. Without a word to either Margaret or me, he climbed up the rungs. "I love you Daddy," I said as I wrapped my arms and legs around him and clung to him as he carried me down. Over his shoulder I glared at Margaret as he sat me down and pried my fingers from his neck. She glared back.

Few children our age lived in our rural neighborhood, so despite Margaret's bossiness, we were still a team. The two kids who did live on our street were not granted the free reign by their parents like Margaret and I enjoyed.

"Let's ask Sherry if she wants to go bike riding with us," Margaret said one a day, knowing we were bored with each other's company. Sherry was my age and lived across the street.

"I have to ask my mom." Sherry twisted a curly lock of blonde hair around her finger.

Margaret straddled her bike and searched the back yard. "Go ask her. Where is she?"

"She'll probably say, no. I have chores." Sherry nodded her head toward the open door of the garden shed. "She's in the shed."

Margaret stepped off her bike, laid it on the ground and faced Sherry. "You want to go don't you?"

Sherry frowned. "Sure. But like I said …"

Margaret grabbed Sherry's hand and tugged her down the sidewalk. "Just shut the door. Lock her in. Come on," Margaret said. "Then we'll take off."

Margaret slammed the door and dropped the latch.

I froze, straddling my bike.

Sherry, too, stood in place, staring at Margaret who was now poking her. "Hurry!' She said. "Get your bike."

Margaret raced to her bike, mounted it, poised to make her escape. I did the same.

Sherry stood by her own bicycle, staring back at the pounding erupting from the shed's locked door. She flinched at each one of her mother's her shouts.

Margaret shook her head and nodded at me. "Let's get out of here."

We raced away. I dared a glance back in time to catch Sherry's mom waving her arms while her daughter pointed in our direction. Sherry was blaming Margaret and me. No surprise.

We didn't slow down until we veered off into the empty lot at the end of the block and hid in a thick grove of trees. Like a team, we dropped our bikes, and clutching our bellies, we collapsed on the ground, rolling with laughter. My big sister was gutsy. Good times.

"Hurry up! Get the salt shaker." Margaret whispered as she held open the back screen door.

I grabbed the shaker, scrambled out the door and took the porch steps two at a time. Fireflies blinked under the black canopy of the elm. I could smell the late afternoon rain still dripping from the leaves. The darkness felt like a damp blanket. The lamp's glow from front room window reached into the street as we ventured across and through the neighbors' unfenced yards.

Margaret aimed the flashlight beam. "Watch out for the rake." The tool rested in the tall grass at the edge of the McAllister's garden. "Come on."

We sat down cross-legged in the garden's moist dirt between the two rows of tomato plants. Margaret plucked a fat tomato, hanging low on the vine, its color such a deep red it appeared black in the moonlight. She pointed to another, "There's a juicy one."

I dug out the salt shaker from my jacket pocket, plucked the fruit from the stem and nibbled the skin away. Dousing the juicy prize with salt, I bit into the tomato as I reached over and salted Margaret's.

The juices dripped from Margaret's mouth as she bit into the tomato. She sat straight-backed and rigid. Pulling out a linen napkin from her pocket, she dabbed at her chin. The night breeze caressed our foreheads. "Let's pretend we're dining at Alexander's Steak House in Chicago," Margaret said. "I read that Nicky Hilton requested buckets of Alexander's salad dressing to be flown to the Anaheim Hilton when he married Liz Taylor."

"Who's Nicky Hilton?"

Margaret shook her head. "Sometimes you are so stupid." With the corner of her pretend linen napkin, she patted the tomatoes juices from the smirk on her face. "Someday I'm going to get out of this small minded town."

CHAPTER FIVE
2015

I kissed Margaret as she slept, turned off the TV. Ronnie Howard and Andy Griffith faded to black. Slipping out the front door, muggy air surrounded me, making my skin clammy. Desert clouds, golden and grey, brooded over the mountains that kept LA's ocean breeze from reaching the inland valley. Instead, the monsoonal wind carried dust and rain. By the time I pulled into the garage, huge droplets dotted the drive. Icy cold pellets soaked my t-shirt when I stepped out of the car to pick up an advertisement which had been thrown on the driveway.

In the house I piled the mail on the desk and padded to my recliner in the living room. Marmalade appeared from one of his cat hidey-holes, and trotted along behind me. I plopped into the chair and sank into its plush cushions. The cat leaped onto my lap, purring and butting his head against my arm. "How you doing, little buddy?" I scratched his ears as he answered with loud soothing purrs. I planted several kisses on his nose, which caused him to jump down in his usual indignant but amusing manner.

The days flipped by like pages of a thick calendar. They weighed on me more and more, the weaker and weaker Margaret became.

I longed for the healing balm of nature which renewed my spirit. I yearned for the indescribable awe of driving through the Rockies with my entire home behind the driver's seat and Marmalade on my lap. I ached to stand speechless before the thundering Niagara Falls, and to soak up the thrill of adventure and the excitement of discovery.

I missed meeting and talking to the locals in every small town, unwrapping their unusual stories and magical histories that would have remained obscure.

After Nate passed away ten years ago I enjoyed the freedom from the constrictions of a relationship. And anyway, Margaret became my go-to person and my best friend. She always had time for me, listening to the events of my day and helping me work through an employee or girlfriend problem. There were never boyfriend problems. I had none.

But lately I wondered if something was wrong with me, as if the world had shifted. I often conducted conversations late at night with Nate's spirit when I couldn't sleep. "Who will have my back after Maggie is gone?" I would ask him. "I don't want to die alone," I told him. "If I am supposed to be with someone, I know you love me, so can you find him for me?"

I never thought Margaret would go before me. She had always been the healthy one. I was the one out of shape. I had only recently quit smoking. Who was going to care for me when I was dying? Margaret suggested I begin to look for a new sister to replace our relationship. "I have a girlfriend who is like a sister to me. But she is not blood. She is only a good friend." I said.

I pulled the Lazy Boy's lever raising the footrest, and leaned back. It would be months before the weather cooled. I recalled last summer's road trip up the coast, standing on a sea cliff along California's Route 1 and listening to the churning surf below as the waves pounded against the rocks.

Marmalade nudged my hand and I returned from my daydreams to my quiet, muggy living room. Outside the motor home waited alongside the house. Except for the food and clothes, my trusty steed was loaded and ready to roll. A shadow of guilt swept over me and I shivered. I can't leave now.

The summer storm thundered outside, rattling the patio doors and promising rain, which would only make the moist heat of southern California more unbearable.

A lightening flash lit up the dim living room. I flipped the recliner's lever, dropping the foot rest, and rose from the chair. Marmalade sprang to the floor. Outside the rain rattled the patio's vinyl roof. Watermelon raindrops danced in the puddles on the concrete, shooting up tiny ringlets of water.

An image of Margaret and me, dancing in the thick grassy ditches across the street from our childhood home, tugged at me. The cold rainwater gave us goose bumps as we ran the length of the culvert, splashing in knee-deep, soft, grassy gutters.

A bass-like boom shook the windows. The memory of my late husband, Nate, entered my mind. He had been gone ten years, but now it felt like yesterday.

The day before he died, a powerful afternoon storm like this one blustered and boomed, rattling my world as if Father Time swept down in search for souls whose time had expired. I smiled, not surprised my Nate gave up his fight and went out with the wind of the storm's aftermath. His life and our relationship had been turbulent and I had been happy all these years making it on my own. But the idea of continuing alone no longer appealed to me.

As I watched the rain, I recalled a vivid dream, some would call a visitation from Nate. I sank back into the memory. Nate stood by a rotted fence. It leaned inland, away from the edge of the windswept ocean cliff as if the old wooden posts knew the danger of falling into the churning surf below.

My heart came alive with surprise at the sight of him. He was twenty-five again twenty-five again. His hair, combed back from his temples, was unaffected by the ocean breeze. He still wore that favorite t-shirt, "Harley Rules." His granddaughter used to tease him because he wore it in every family photo. "Is that the only shirt you own?" She had asked.

I rushed to him. "Nate! It's been so long. I've missed you."

"I've been very busy."

"That's good," I said. He had never been social sort. He seemed happier.

We sat down in the lush grass and leaned against the picket fence.

"Everyone wonders what happened to you." I said. "They think we got a divorce."

We both chuckled, remembering how our friends at the 12-step program reacted when they found out we had ran off to Vegas and gotten married. They had formed a betting pool as to how long our marriage would last.

The early years of our marriage had been tumultuous. I'd pressed charges because of his jealousy and abuse. We divorced only to work it out a year later and enjoy a comfortable relationship. We never remarried.

I glanced at the coastal fog clinging to the rotting fence posts lining the cliff's edge. Like the leaning timbered posts, Nate and I had weathered the storms, too.

He threw a crooked smile at me and it fluttered across my heart strings like a song.

"I've missed you so much," I said again.

Nate, stood to go. His once perfect slicked back hair now tussled by the wind. Knowing our time was up, I found it hard to breathe. I wanted to touch him. To hold him. To kiss him a thousand times. But I didn't do any of those things. "Don't go."

He leaned down to me. His fingers lifted my chin up, forcing my sad eyes to focus on his hypnotizing clear blue ones. The music of pounding surf and the seagulls singing their songs faded away, "You can come with me," he said."

The idea startled me. I jumped up. A strong desire to take his suggestion shot through me and then left just as abruptly. "I can't!!

Uncontrolled sobs erupted from deep within me. "I can't!! I can't!!" His words stirred up an army of emotions as if pushing me to take the leap, to surrender.

If I said yes, we could be together forever. He had changed. This time the relationship would be better than we could ever have imagined.

"I can't! I can't! I gulped in breaths of air and awoke, thrashing the bed covers. Nate was gone. It was only a dream. I was still in our bed in California.

As I lay in bed trying to shake off the dregs of the dream's hold on me, my cell vibrated inside my jean pocket. Fishing it out, I recognized Margaret's number. "Hi Maggie." I said. "What do you need?"

I heard her tsk tsk because I called her Maggie, but she said nothing. "Did you water the plants on the patio?"

"No, I didn't. Can't you get Daniel or Michael to do it? They're coming tomorrow."

"I hate to ask them to do anything. They're so busy with the kids and work and everything. Anyway, I'm not sure Michael is even coming. He said if his dad decides to show up, then he's not going to come."

I rolled my eyes. I guess it's okay to ask me to do everything, I thought. I took a deep breath. "I'll do it Sunday."

"But you're coming Saturday for dinner aren't you?"

I sighed. I wanted — I needed a day off. Nate had never been this demanding. "What time are they coming? "

"I never ask. Probably around ten. They'll call me when they're leaving L.A."

They arrived at noon.

I exchanged the expected hugs with the daughter-in-laws, while Michael's toddler banged a wooden spoon on the coffee table. I peeked down the hall. Margaret's bedroom door was closed. I looked up at Michael, questioning.

"Daniel's with her. Dad's on his way."

Reaching out, I rubbed his shoulder. "I'm glad you put your feelings aside about your dad and decided to come." He uttered a disgusted snort and stepped away from my touch. "This day is about your mom, not about you," I said.

He assumed a wide stance, crossed his arms and glared at me. A spark fired in his eyes. "It's stupid that he even wants to come. It's been twenty-five years. I would not be all emotional over my ex-wife after 25 years."

"Really, Michael?" I wanted to slap him. "You forget they had twenty-eight years together. She's the mother of his children. Come back and tell me how stupid you think it is when you and Tonya have shared almost thirty years of marriage, through deaths and sickness and children."

I spun around, walked outside and plopped down on the patio swing. Pulling my phone from my pocket, I busied myself, checking in with Facebook friends and going through emails. I waited until I heard additional voices at the front door, and then came back inside to greet Simon and his wife, Ingrid.

Simon's red hair had thinned and faded long ago, but he was fit. His thick arms bowed away from his torso, evidence of the many hours he spent at his in-home gym, which was stocked with equipment which rivaled a 24-Hour Fitness. His wife, Ingrid, who was always preparing for some Iron Man event across the country, made a habit of working out beside him. Her lithe, tanned sixty-year old body showed no signs of age.

Simon had not divorced Margaret, she had divorced him. It may have been twenty-five years ago, but I believed he was still in love wth my sister.

"You know he's still in love with you?" I told Margaret once. She only shrugged, as if she doubted the statement.

"Maybe," she had said. "The fact he cheated on me more than once doesn't seem to be an issue in his mind." She pressed her lips together as if to hold back, what? Then, she waved her hand in dismissal. I guessed many resentments boiled just under her skin.

I am forever the romantic. I hugged Simon. Whatever happened, it was long past. Right or wrong, affairs or not. I understood. The man believed he loved my sister.

Pulling back from our embrace, Simon's face screwed up with emotion, his moist eyes crinkled at the corners. He frowned at me with concern. "How're you doing?" He asked.

His genuine caring struck a chord. No one in the family had asked me that question. Certainly not my nephews nor their wives. "I'm holding up. Thanks." I swiped at my own tears.

Time was running out for my sister.

After the greetings, Margaret moved from her bedroom to the patio swing outside, and her family entourage followed. Michael hung back with me in the kitchen as I poured a glass of ice water for Margaret. "I told Daniel I thought we could pick up burgers from Carl's Jr.," he said. "Daniel said he wasn't sure that's what everyone wanted." He looked at his watch. "I'm still waiting for an answer."

I couldn't temper my voice. "Just make a decision, Michael." Could he not even be assertive about a meal?

I recalled my conversation with Margaret yesterday when Margaret requested I oversee the family visit.

"Could you ask Simon and Ingrid to leave after lunch?" She had asked me.

I paused, not knowing what to say. "What do you mean?"

"I'm afraid Simon might hang around after everyone else goes home and I don't want to be alone with him."

Why would Margaret want me to handle her family dynamics? She rarely welcomed me in her circles, but I guessed she knew the feeling was mutual. I never held a desire to be a part of her L.A. image of propriety. And now she was asking me to tell her family what to do?

So it began. The death watch began to unravel convoluted family dynamics. Like trash swept under a Persian carpet, the unscripted, and sleeping issues awakened, crawling their way out into the open.

"Why can't you just say you're tired? Play the cancer card?" I asked.

Margaret shook her head. "He might argue. He's never listened to me. The idea of dealing with him makes me want to throw up."

"But me? Why don't you ask Daniel?"

"I don't want him to get in an argument with his dad."

"Okay, I will. It's not that I mind." I was foolishly flattered that she trusted me to handle what to her was a delicate matter. "It's not that complicated. I'll just say you're tired and need to rest. Which will be true anyway."

The afternoon, still humid from yesterday's storm, wore on. Margaret played out her hostess role, enduring the family chatter which used to bring her joy. Someone must have decided on Mexican food. Simon and Ingrid went home without being asked, and the boys and their families said their good byes shortly after. Once more, Margaret carried out her performance until her last guest left.

CHAPTER SIX
1954

Immigrants didn't have the luxury of dwelling on they felt, they were too busy surviving. My parents followed the lead of their Irish-German immigrant parents, reading the scripts handed down to them.

Arguments and anger were never written into the dialogue. A stiff politeness was the rule. Like an understudy, I followed Mom and Dad's lead. Constraint in our tiny home was the norm. If emotions dared to flare, Dad claimed a migraine and retreated to the bedroom which Mom no longer shared with him.

I was eight. I sat cross-legged on the floor in the living room, erecting an elaborate cabin from the heap of

Lincoln logs in front of me. Rain beat against the picture window.

I looked up as Mom stomped into the room, her hair damp from her trek to the mailbox at the end of our drive. Wiping her hands, she jerked the mail from her apron pocket and tossed it onto the small desk in the corner of the room. Spinning around, she glared down at me. "If I divorce your dad, who're you going to live with?"

Her anger startled me.I knew my answer mattered to her. "I don't know," I said.

"Well, you better decide." She stormed out of the room.

I wrestled with my decision for days. I loved both of my parents. A continual sadness floated over Dad, like the dust cloud hovering over Linus in the Carl Shultz' cartoons. I made my decision. My father needed me more. When Mom pressed for an answer I said, "I'll live with Dad."

Her soft lips disappeared into a thin line. "You always were a daddy's girl." She spat out the words, dousing my well thought out decision as if it were a wild fire and stormed from the room. Her words cracked, snapping like a whip. I felt their sting.

Although confused by her anger, her hurt became mine. From that moment on, I kept my own counsel. Huddling in the comfortable seclusion of my closet became my favorite pastime. In the low light of a desk lamp, I lay on my belly, knees bent, ankles crossed, reading my books, The Black Stallion Returns, Black Beauty, and My Friend Flicka.

I wrote my feelings in my diary which no one wanted to hear —my simplest thoughts and biggest dreams. I dreamed of being like my heroes, The Lone Ranger, Gene Autry or Roy Rogers. I wanted to make people feel better, solve their problems and then ride away, across the open range, enjoying the freedom of the open spaces.

At times mom's muffled crying crept out from her bed pillow, under the closet door and into the alcove of clothes where I read my books and wrote my thoughts. Her pain pulled at me. Tip toeing into her room, I crawled up beside her. Wiping her tears, she rolled over to face me, "What do you want Janice?"

I held her hand, led her to my bedroom and pointed to the makeshift shingle which I had scribbled and hung on my closet door. I read my sign aloud. "Counseling." "I will help you feel better," I said. With a heart full of innocence and good will, I believed I could make it so.

"How're you ever going to solve mine and your dad's problems when I can't?" Once again, her sharp words cut me down, as if she had slapped me.

If she cried after that, I never heard her, which relieved me because her sadness distressed me and because she convinced me I could not help.

I resorted to a fantasy world. I imagined I was a wild stallion, galloping through the house on all fours. My knees became calloused. Like my heroes, I rode free across the wide-open prairie, down the hall and through the living room.

Eventually Mom swallowed her sullen behavior and made a turn around. She became driven. Most nights, after we cleared the dinner table and homework was done, Mom, Margaret and I spent the evening assembling kits, which Mom had ordered from the Tandy Leather catalog. She oversaw our work as we stitched pre-cut pieces of leather together, creating soft, suede moccasins, squaw belts, men's belts, and women's pixie bags. It was family time to me, but one day I asked, "Why are we doing this?"

"Your father told me if I divorce him I will never get any of his money. I don't want you girls to be like me. Don't ever be dependent on a man. Be independent." We created enough product to fill two old, scarred suitcases which we strapped into our bicycle handlebars and headed out around the neighborhood to hawk our wares. Lugging my suitcase up to the front door of every house, I cracked it open and recited our sales pitch which I remember to this day. "Would you like to buy any belts, moccasins, or pixie bags?"

When we were younger — too young for our Tandy Leather business — we still earned money. Mom drove us out to the lake early Saturday and Sunday mornings in search of soda pop bottles, to redeem. A nickel or dime a bottle was easy money for young girls.

Another of Mom's moneymaking schemes was collecting rags. She dropped us off in a nice neighborhood and parked at the corner while Margaret and I canvassed from door to door asking, "Do you have any old clothes or rags that you don't need?" Almost everyone disappeared into their house and returned with armfuls. I am sure they thought us beggars. When our bags were stuffed to their limit, Mom pulled up and we dragged them to the curb. Tossing our bounty into the back of her station wagon, Mom handed us another empty bag.

The local newspaper purchased our bags of rags for fifteen cents a pound which they used to clean their presses. So at the end of the day, Mom hauled our catch to the Springfield Illinois Journal and sent us up to pound loudly on the back door until a stocky man answered, his clothes, his hands and even his face stained with ink. He rolled up a big door, grabbed our bags of rags one by one from the car and threw them onto a large scale. "Seventy-five pounds," he announced as we sat eagerly waiting on the station wagon's tailgate. "You girls worked hard today," he said. We beamed as he counted out the $11.25 bounty.

Money meant independence, and independence meant freedom, mom said. By the time we were ten and eleven we were feeding a healthy savings account. What I didn't save for my dream horse, I spent on comic books and records.

One day as Margaret and I pedaled home from school, the lure of barking dogs filtered out from a garage at the end of a long drive. The dogs' calls became like a marching song, leading us down the long driveway toward the sign, Ed Bracy Kennels.

Mr. Bracey, a highly esteemed dog handler and celebrated judge for the American Kennel Club Dog Show circuit, had converted his two-car garage into a kennel to house the dogs he groomed and showed professionally.

We pedaled up the drive and dismounted as the barking rose to a crescendo. Portable fencing reached across the garage's open door. Behind the wired barrier a slim man with thick peppery hair bent over a huge white, fluffy dog lying prone on a grooming table. He didn't look up, concentrating on his work. A brush in his hand, his arm moved back and forth with slow steady strokes across the dog's white cottony coat. Occasionally he patted the dog's head.

We walked up to the gate. "Hi," I shouted over the din of the barking dogs.

He looked up from his project and swiped his forehead with his arm, the dog brush still in his hand. His deep tan appeared even darker in contrast against his bleached white T-shirt. Smiling, he set the brush on the table and rubbed his hands on his jeans. "Hello girls. Where do you live?"

I had to raise my voice over the dogs' outburst. "Down the street." I pointed. "Third house from the end," I said. "What are you doing?"

The man's hair, mostly black with highlights of silver-white streaks laid snug against his head, unmoved by the afternoon breeze floating through the kennel. Tufts of dog hair swirled in the aisle between the wall cages and the cyclone fencing of the exercise runs.

The dog on his table jumped to its feet and shook. Its ears slapped against its clean shaven nose and the long white fluffy fur on its head flopped over his eyes. We laughed as the dog licked the man's shadow beard. "Can he see with that hair in his eyes?"

"I'm going to tie it up." He combed up the hair like I did my ponytail and wrapped and twisted a cloth covered elastic band around it. The dog licked his face again and he laughed along with us.

"Is it a girl or a boy? What's his name?"…..

Dogs and puppies were a sure cure for after school boredom. The kennel became a regular stop for Margaret and I as we discovered a new world — the back stage of dog show competition. Every day we hung out, sweeping dog runs and observing the tedious grooming process necessary for a dog to become a champion in the show ring. On weekends, we clambered out of bed at daybreak to arrive for the morning feeding and returned late afternoon for the second. We washed dog dishes, cleaned runs and soon learned to brush and bathe dogs. There was a Mrs. Bracey who brought us iced tea and muffins. And

I imagined we two little girls, with energy and time on their hands, filled a hole in the Bracey's childless marriage. They took to us, like we took to the dogs.

No longer answering only to ourselves, we learned to take responsibility and direction from this kindly mentor. As the months passed, we blossomed with the illusive confidence of youth. One day, finished with our chores, we hung around watching Mr. Bracey treat the dry brittle coat of a standard poodle for an upcoming show. The contented dog lay on its side atop the grooming crate. He brushed up sections of the dog's coat one at a time, dousing each tuft with baby oil. The process was slow — and boring. Margaret shoved me for no reason and I pushed her back. We began to horse around until my foot snagged Mr. Bracey's clipper cord, sending the tool to crash to the concrete garage floor, cracking the casing.

We froze. My stomach clenched into a knot and my throat squeezed so tight I couldn't swallow. I couldn't breathe. My tongue stuck to the roof of my dry mouth. All my pride and good feelings drained from me, puddling at my feet.

Margaret's words penetrated the buzzing in my ears. "We're sorry," she said. She handed Mr. Bracey the broken clippers. I stood, glued in place, unable to move.

My shoulders sank and I hung my head. I recalled when Mr. Bracey and his wife had invited us to go with them for the weekend to a dog show. The trip became a series of firsts — first to stay in a motel, our first dog show, and with the biggest experience of all, the first with no parents.

Margaret's big sister skills kicked in. In our motel room she stood before me, straightening my collar and checking my hair, before we left to join the Bracey's for breakfast. "Make sure you eat all your eggs," she instructed.

I shoved her away. "Why?" I asked as I picked up my purse. "I don't eat the whites at home."

"Margaret primped in the mirror. "You can't be picky. You have to act like a lady. And remember the napkin goes on your lap."

They're probably waiting on us," I said and headed out the door.

That weekend when I arrived home, in spite of being weary of Margaret's constant fussing, I stood taller. I hadn't had a birthday, I was still twelve, but I felt all grown up.

Now it was all gone. Mr. Bracey examined the clippers and laid them aside. He didn't even look at us. The pride, the confidence and the respect we had earned. Gone. His clipped words slipped through the tight thin line of his lips, "I think you two should go home."

CHAPTER SEVEN
2015

Margaret's illness progressed. The boys visited more often and I, too, made more of an effort. I scheduled my travel schedule so I would be in town for most holidays, her birthday and when her sons came. "I am so happy you could make it," Margaret would always say to me.

Shortly after Margaret bought her home in Sun City she planned a house warming barbeque, inviting the boys and their families. Margaret's ex, Simon, never wanted to miss out on family time with his sons and grandchildren, so he aways insisted on an invite. I believed he also did not want to miss out on an excuse to see Margaret.

Simon had ruled their twenty-eight marriage with a dominating and abrasive manner from which Margaret always backed down until one day when Margaret pressed him about an affair she believed he was having. She pushed him too far. The argument became violent and he threatened her with one of his many guns. It was then she was forced to find the courage to divorce him.

Even after all these years everyone adhered to the unspoken family rule, "Don't upset Simon." During most of the family functions, Simon's opinions were never questioned and his actions were never challenged.

On this particular day at the house warming and barbque, Michael's toddler wandered out of sight. Michael shouted at his father. "Where's Benny? You're supposed to be watching him while I cook the hamburgers."

"I am watching him!"

"No you're not! "

Like a flash fire, emotions flared up and Simon puffed up, ready to prove his fatherly authority. "Don't talk to me like that!"

Margaret sat on the patio swing with a forced calmness and tight-lipped. She said nothing. Did no one respect this was her home? She didn't need this. The neighbors' open windows meant they, too, could hear. My face heated with embarrassment for Margaret and for me. This was my family, too. These neighbors were my friends and customers. Stunned,

I listened as the boys and their dad shouted back and forth.

They thought I was the redneck sister? I was not going to have Margaret's neighbors witness her family — no, my family — disrespecting my sister on my watch.

I jumped from my chair and shouted over the raised voices. "Stop it!"

Startled faces swung around in my direction, every mouth agape. I had their attention.

"This is not going to happen here!" My eyes swept the crowd meeting every one's shocked expression. "Your mother doesn't need this. Take the argument somewhere else or drop it."

Heads swiveled to Margaret who only raised her brows but did not discount me. Like a water hose at a dog fight, their ruffled fur lay down. Someone tittered at a joke I couldn't hear.

Margaret possessed no courage for confrontation. I whispered a silent thank you to my Nate whose own blustery and abrasive attitude had pushed me to confront him and even have him arrested when he became abusive. Because of him, I learned to stand up for myself and, in turn, earned his respect.

From then on, Margaret insisted on my presence at the functions which Simon usually attended but no other flare ups occurred. I became her insurance, or better, her bouncer. But still, I was ignored, like a low-key presidential FBI agent with the buzz haircut and

Ray Ban sunglasses who provided security at an event.

Margaret was having one of her better days as she and her boys and their families filed into Margaret's favorite Mexican restaurant, The children settled in, the little ones with coloring books and the oldest with her iPad.

Questions, never directed at me, batted back and forth over the menus. 'What do you want? What're you going to get?'

Quiet and controlled, Margaret sat at the end of the table. It occurred to me now she always presented this demeanor. My memory of her when she was nine flashed in my mind. She sat in the garden dirt, the glow of her flashlight illuminating her crossed legs, as she sat straight backed, dabbing the tomato juices dripping down her chin.

Today the family chattered amongst themselves ordering their food, I sat back, sipping my coffee. When the food had been served and the table chatter lulled, I broke my silence. "Michael, how's the remodel job coming along?"

"I hope to complete it within the next two weeks."

Margaret and I had visited his project during the demolition stage. "I would love to see it finished." I said.

At the other end of the table, Daniel wiped up a spill in front of his youngest. "How about you, Daniel?" I asked. "How's life treating you?"

"Work is work," Daniel said as he offered his two-year old a tortilla chip to suck on. "Denise and I have to get up so early to get the kids to day care, catch the train to work in the city, and then I pick them up because Denise always works late. When she gets home I have dinner ready and then it's to bed and then do it all over again the next day."

Denise, who played the silent invisible role, worked the long hours required to become a partner at the law firm where she worked.

"No one ever said work was fun," I said. "That's why they call it work."

Kids today. I'd experienced the same mind set in my teens but grew out of it. These days things are different. I'd experienced the same attitude at my pet salon the last few years before I finally sold it. at my pet grooming shop. Long hours and hard work seemed to be a violation of human rights. The difficulty in finding loyal, hardworking employees had become the final straw which eventually pushed me to sell the business.

"You can come work for me," Michael tossed the competitive challenge at his brother with a smirk, knowing his brother wouldn't stoop to contract labor.

Daniel didn't pick up the gauntlet and for distraction I turned to him and said, "Margaret tells me you're tackling writing a novel."

Daniel grinned boyishly and shoved a forkful of beans and rice into his mouth. "I'm working on it."

I nodded in understanding and waited for the conversation to expand, but instead Michael joined in. "A friend of mine just received a $10,000.00 bonus for his book, Grazing *in L.A.* It's about finding edible foods growing in downtown L.A." Daniel stabbed at his salad. .

No one inquired about my books on Amazon, or what I was working on at the moment. The meal wore on. Their lack of interest did not surprise me. After all, I am a –published author. I have no degrees, I live in the boondocks of the Inland Empire. And I am not from L.A.

The conversation turned to the baby's progress in potty training and the eight year old's latest science project. After lunch we returned to the house and enjoyed a beautiful California afternoon outside on the patio. The children marched back and forth across the mock wooden bridge, which arched over the simulated pebble creek. Someone dragged out the wading pool and Tonya took on the role of playground monitor.

Conversations remained light with nothing directed to me. I followed suit, just as I had done, huddled in my childhood bedroom closet, writing in my diary and getting lost in my books. Whatever I had to say was of no interest to this family. I was not a part of this L.A. family.

I longed to get on the road. In my mind I was already gone. And I was already alone.

CHAPTER EIGHT
1960

Owning up to our careless actions at the kennels felt a hundred times worse than being called out for talking in class. Mom pulled into the Bracey's driveway and waited as we slinked out of the car. No longer feeling privileged to use the back door, we stared at the ground and marched up to the Bracey's front entrance. Like outcasts, we knocked. Mr. and Mrs. Bracey invited us in and we cowered in the foyer. Margaret clutched the envelope in her hand.

The couple loomed before us. "Did you girls have something to say?"

I glanced at Margaret, who was frozen in place. I snatched the envelope from her and thrust it out into the large gap between the Bracey's and us. "Here." I said. " We want to pay for the clippers."

Mr. Bracey took it and opened it. The envelope held all of our savings, eighty-five dollars. The silence echoed across the canyon between us. Margaret's elbow nudged me. I jumped as if startled, and then remembered the speech mom had helped us rehearse. My words spewed out. "I am sorry. I should not have been playing around. I hope the money will be enough. Please let us know." I gasped for a breath. I motioned to Margaret. Her pale face, like stone, focused on her feet, the creases on her forehead, too deep for a little girl. She slowly looked up at the couple before her. "I'm …I mean…. we're sorry, Mr. and Mrs. Bracey." Margaret swung her attention to me with a pleading look. I nodded in encouragement. She looked back to the Bracey's. "We were careless. I hope you'll forgive us and let us come back. It will never happen again."

During the following weeks, we dealt with the consequences of our carelessness. Forgiven, we were again allowed to hang out at the kennels, although our time there was limited. We stayed busy selling our belts, moccasins and pixie bags to earn back the money we had withdrawn from our savings. Months later, during a quiet time in the kennel when the dogs dozed after their morning feeding, Mr.

Bracey and his wife sat us down and announced they were moving to Mississippi.

"I suggested to your mother that we could refer all our retired show dogs to you girls and you could take over grooming them," Mr. Bracey said. "If I know your mother, she's probably clearing out the coal room in the basement right now." He smiled at his wife. "What do you say girls? Are you ready to start up your own business?"

Our heads bobbed in unison. "Sure!"

The door that had slammed in our faces months before now swung open with the promise of a new adventure. We picked out the paint colors, mom ordered clippers, combs, and brushes, and the Bracey's donated a couple old grooming show crates. A radio was the last accessory. On weekends, as we groomed, our voices echoed off the cinderblock walls and drifted out the open door of the coal chute. We belted out Elvis', *You Ain't Nothin' But A Hound Dog*, Paul Anka's, *Put Your Head On My Shoulder,* and my favorite, Annette Funicello's, *Where The Boys Are*, drowning out the hum of the clippers. The Canine Beauty Salon was in full operation.

The clientele we inherited from Mr. Bracey which frequented our back door included the Mayor's schnauzer, and various breeds of dogs belonging to politicians and local business people. Tips were big. When Illinois winters coated the roads with ice and snow, making it dangerous driving, our canine appointments arrived by cab, unaccompanied by their owners.

Margret and I spent our weekends in the converted coal room. We sang to fifties tunes while Margaret directed the operation of bathing and grooming the dogs, usually numbering ten each day. We averaged a plush $5.00 an hour. Mom insisted we deposit half of the income into our savings and the balance increased steadily over the next several years. When we turned fifteen and sixteen, the next-door neighbor mentioned he was moving his family to California.

"I think you girls should invest your savings and buy the house next door. What do you think?" Mom slid our breakfast plates in front of us. It really wasn't a question. Mom's mind was made up.

Margaret and I looked at one another and shrugged.

"We'll sell the property when you go to college." Mom's mind was made up. She managed our aspiring business, booking appointments throughout the entire weekends. The two sisters who had played together as children, now worked together. She left us no time for taunting neighborhood kids or arguments amongst ourselves. She banked half the grooming money we earned and the other half we made the payment on the house and the rest left over meant we no longer had to accept the clothes mom brought home from the Goodwill and Salvation Army.

"Do you want to go shopping after we clean up?" I swept up the dog hair and scooped it into the trash. "I can't wait to go to Meyers Bros."

"No, let's go to Barker's. The quality's better," Margaret said. "Though we're never going to get the best unless we get out of Springfield and go shopping in Chicago."

"I don't think we'll be going to Chicago any time soon."

"I'm getting my driver's permit next month," Margaret said as she switched off the radio and turned off the lights.

I followed Margaret as we climbed up the basement stairs. "Do you really think Mom and Dad are going to let you drive to Chicago?"

CHAPTER NINE
2015

Like the cancer, the months wore on. Margaret's weakness increased with each passing day and the disease's strength grew like an unstoppable monster. It stood at the foot of her bed, pounding its chest in defiance. But Margaret was neither a quitter, nor a whiner. When her boys visited, she called upon her thin string of strength and attempted to hide the progression of the disease.

I slipped the key in the lock, took a deep breath and opened the front door. The shadows of the dimly lit house, like fog on a dark night, hid the heavy atmosphere, but I smelled it. The shroud was thickest in the bedroom.

I found Margaret sitting up, clutching a bowl of cereal in her lap with pillows propped behind her, "I've had a bad morning," she said as soon I entered. "After Gus left, when as I was taking a shower, I started vomiting. The colostomy bag came loose. It was a mess. I felt faint so I laid down right there. I must have passed out. I came to, shivering with cold water beating down on me."

"Oh dear! Are you okay now?" I stepped into the bathroom and pulled back the curtain. The shower was clean. "You cleaned it up?"

"I didn't want the health care worker to find the mess."

"You should've called me." Her undignified situation tore at my heart. E of this was her style of living. I straightened the covers and checked her bedside table. "I'll get you some fresh water."

"I'm okay. I just ate too much last night. I'm fine now." She scooped up the last spoonful of cereal from her bowl. "But would you spray some air freshener in the bathroom?"

Lately, she liked to blame every bad day on what she ate or how much. "What did you eat last night?"

"Gus fixed me a bowl of soup and a roll. I even had a piece of pie that pie the neighbor brought over yesterday."

I thought you had soup the night before?"

I watched Margaret struggle with the timeline. She held up her appointment book, studying her meticulous notes, her pain levels, the times she took her pills, their dosages and what she ate. "That's right," she said. "Last night Gus brought home Mexican."

The cancer had escalated its rampage and the dosage of OxyContin increased. Bad days came more often. Margaret admitted she never wanted to eat, but she forced herself. Either because she believed as her son did, that her only problem was her weight loss, or because she feared Michael's wrath for not eating. Either way, my throat tightened from the urgency of her daily downward spiral. I choked back tears.

 "You shouldn't be taking a shower alone. Why don't you take it before Gus leaves so he will be here if you need help?"

Seven years ago, after Margaret's initial diagnosis, surgery, chemo and radiation, her L.A. doctors declared her cancer free from the stage four ovarian cancer. Upon the good news, she moved out of her son's guest house in L.A. and purchased a house in the Inland Empire, only a mile from me.

She preferred L.A, but couldn't afford to buy there. "This is going to be great," I told her. "We'll be BFFs. We can go shopping and hiking, and out to lunch. We'll go to the pool, too." We were more than sisters, she was my confidant. Margaret, who had never lived alone, poured herself into the decorating and landscaping.

She was outside in the back doing yard work. I found her on her on her knees by the walk, shadowed by her wide brimmed sun hat and pulling weeds. "I just stopped by to tell you the community center is having a 50's dance at the senior center tonight. Do you want to go?"

She straightened. Rolling back on her heels, she wiped her forehead and gave me a silly smile. "Sure. Why not?"

"Good! We'll cut up and do the jitterbug, It'll be fun."

Several men asked her to dance. Gus had been one of them. I remembered him as a customer who brought his dog into my pet salon for grooming. They danced an entire set, exchanged phone numbers, and their relationship began — A loving relationship nothing like the twenty-eight year abrasive one she had experienced with Simon. Gus was a soft-spoken, humble man, everything Simon, her boys, and her L.A. friends were not. The romance flourished.

For six weeks Margaret lived her life, relishing in Gus's attentive, loving behavior and living in contentment and the security of her new home. She decorated, cooked and tended to her garden. But six weeks later, when the doctors delivered the results of her follow up tests, they gave Margaret the dire news. Her cancer had returned.

Gus had lost three wives in his lifetime, the last one to ovarian cancer, like Margaret. When Margaret gave him the somber news, she said "Our relationship is new, you can break this off now," she told him. "I will understand."

I came by the following morning, curious about how he had taken the news. Margaret met me at the door with emotional watery eyes. "After I told him, he leaned in and kissed me. Then he said, 'I'm not going anywhere. Now, let's go to dinner, you've had a rough day."

Gus remained a steady force throughout the past seven years of Margaret's battle. He filled his days with the various demands of his own home, his other properties and his family. The days Margaret did not drive into LA. To work, he would take her out for dinner or Margaret would cook. They spent their evenings cuddled in bed, watching TV. Every morning Gus kissed her good day, attended Catholic mass and then filled his day with various projects around his house and his children's, who lived nearby. Margaret's regular and comfortable routine with Gus, along with her accounting work and cancer treatments left little time for me.

Gus was the best thing that could have happened to Margaret at this time in her life, yet inside I struggled my irrational jealousy at bay.. With Margaret in a relationship, I was on my own again.

The day came when her L.A. doctors at Cedars Sinai Medical Center gave her the dire news they could do no more for her. They recommended hospice. She gave up her accounting clients and no longer made the drive into L.A.

I posted on Facebook my sister had gone on hospice. Another phase in the death watch began.

My cell dinged constantly with notifications of prayers and well wishes from friends, fans and readers.

I scrolled down to a notification from a name I didn't recognize. A Brent Dickerson had messaged me. *"Mom, could you tell me what is wrong with my Aunt Sandy?"*

"Listen to this. It's weird. " I said to Margaret. I read the message to her. "I don't know who this guy is. Probably a scammer, but it kind of creeps me out."

CHAPTER TEN
1960

The summer months whizzed by as it does for young girls coming of age. Our grooming business thrived. Money was never a problem. I took up horseback riding lessons, and went trail riding whenever I could, spending many hours and much of my grooming money exploring the lush green pastures and rolling, tree covered hills surrounding the stables. Margaret began going steady with a boy from high school and we spent little time together except when we were in the basement grooming.

"Pick me up at five," I shouted as Mom dropped me off at the stables. I slammed the car door and waved as her Rambler station wagon eased around the circular drive.

As Mom's car crept down the long drive I sprinted toward the barn.

A girl my age, deep in concentration, curried and brushed a tall roan tied to the hitching post. His coat and mane glistened in the sun. The girl's sun-bleached hair, tussled by the breeze, hung over her brows, shielding her eyes. As I approached she stepped back, pushed her hair off her forehead and wiped away the sweat on her brow. She ran a hand over the red's gleaming coat and smiled at me.

"Hi," I said. I touched the horse's velvety nose.

"His name's Red," she said.

"Is he yours?" I asked. I'd been coming around the stables every weekend for months. But hadn't noticed the horse.

"Yes. I just got him." She laughed. "I've been begging for a horse since I was five." She ran her fingers through Red's mane. "Isn't he pretty?"

"He sure is," I said.You're so lucky. I've wanted a horse since before I can remember, too, but I don't think my folks will ever buy me one. I'm saving up for one though." I pointed to the palomino standing at the pasture gate. "I rent him every time I come. They call him Trigger. I ride every weekend."

"He's pretty, like Roy Rogers' horse," she said as she set the brush and curry comb on a bale of hay. "I'm Barbara."

"I'm Janice."

"Are you going to ride today?" Barbara asked. "We could ride together."

"Sure! I usually ride in the pasture." I said.

"I'll tell them you're going to ride with me. Then we can go off the property. It'll be fun. There's a pond about a mile from here. It's a really neat place."

That was it. Two young girls with a love of horses sealed their friendship.

The words from my books which had painted pictures of wild, powerful steeds, hooves pounding the ground, and of manes flowing and tails caught by the wind – they all became a reality for this young girl who only had one rule to follow, "Be home by dark."

I raced my Trigger alongside Barbara and her horse. We traveled so fast it felt as if I were flying. I was one with Trigger, like Alec and the Black Stallion. Hours of riding with Barbara only strengthened our friendship. Mom's dreams for me had come true as well. I was free, independent, and living my dreams.

Freedom and independence can be a double-edged sword for a teenage girl. You know how girls get when they turn sixteen? When we weren't horseback riding, we talked about boys.

Back at Barbara's house, behind her closed bedroom door, we sat cross-legged on her bed, facing one another. We laughed and whispered about the boys we knew. We wanted to be ready if one of us got lucky enough to score a date, so we leaned toward each other until our lips met. Then jerked away, falling backwards, we shrieked with silliness.

"That's not how it's done. Do you think?" Barbara asked as she sat up. "I think it should be longer."

I jumped off the bed. "I'm not going to kiss you longer," I said as we both laughed and I paced around the room. "We need a real guy."

Barbara hung her head. "Yeah, I guess you're right. Fat chance though. Where we gonna get one?"

I pushed through the high school doors and crossed the street. Approaching Dad's Jeep, I surveyed the parking spaces at the Java Café on the corner. The rusted out 56 Buick, the blue Plymouth and the Triumph motorcycle filled three of the five spaces. At the coffee shop's entrance two boys, leathered up with chains dangling from their hip pockets, huddled around two girls. Both girls puckered their heavily painted red lips as talked. Their short skirts ended well above the knees. I hadn't seen them in any of my classes, they were probably dropouts. Mom called girls who that looked like that 'wild.' "They're easy," she always said. "They'll end up with a hassle of babies and a deadbeat for a husband.z' She pointed."Like that boy leaning up against his motorcycle."

I didn't care. I'd already asked around. His name was Gary. The boys with the two sluts were his friends, Larry and Chris. Gary leaned against his Triumph. Every day I searched the alley for him. And every day, there he was, his narrow hips propped against his bike, his lanky legs crossed at the ankles.

He sucked in a deep drag from his own cigarette as he focused on the chattering students spewing forth from the building. His leather jacket gaped open, exposing a bleach-white t-shirt. Catching the sunlight, his class ring dangled from a gold chain around his neck, proving no girl had his ring. He was not going steady. I wondered who he waited for. He raked his fingers through his hair and swept it back from his temple.

Barbara's voice, pulled me from my musings. "Hey Janice!" Her Angora sweater clung to her lithe body as she raised her arm and waved. Her pleated skirt reached just below her knees. "We're going to the rink tonight," she said. "You going?" She approached her parent's black Lincoln and pulled open the door.

I waved back. "Sure, later." I said as I climbed into Dad's Willys Jeep.

Margaret, already settled in the back seat, had dropped her stack of books beside her and was berating Dad. "I told you to park down at the end of the block." Everytime, Dad picked us up, she complained. "Why didn't you bring the Desoto?" She whined. "No one drives a Jeep." She hated the jeep.

Dad eyed his eldest daughter in the rearview mirror, shifted gears, and merged into the alley's congested parent traffic. He waited at the stop sign in front of the Java Café for the crossing street traffic to clear. I studied the scene at the Café.

One of the skimpy-skirted girls with a cigarette between her ruby lips leaned forward toward Chris. Her long black hair draped down, hiding her face like a curtain as the redheaded boy lit her cigarette.

Slut number one threw her head back, inhaled deeply, and exhaled into Chris's face, The girl smiled at him. He laughed, waving away the smoke. The two boys exchanged words and Chris threw a playful punch against his buddy's bicep.

Gary, still leaning against his bike, tossed his cigarette, stood and ground the butt with his boot, then waved at his buddies. "See ya. Gotta go."

The boys nodded as Gary threw his leg over his motorcycle. His boot kicked the lever and the engine choked, sputtered and roared to life. My own heart fluttered as the bike spat, blowing blue smoke from its pipes.

The machine growled. Its rear tire spit gravel as he sped down the alley.

Dad edged the Jeep onto the street traffic. The three of us rarely conversed on the drive home. Margaret escaped into her latest library book. Dad steered the Jeep as it crept along in the heavy school traffic.I scanned the sidewalk for my friend, Tamara, When I caught sight of her short-cropped, blonde hair I rolled down the window. "See you at the rink, tonight?"

Tamara's arms crossed her chest as she clutched her books. She searched for the source of my voice, then waved. "I'll be there."

I shot a big smile at Dad. "Can we give her a ride?" He pulled to the curb.

Tamara rushed up to the Jeep, shouting over her shoulder to her companion, "Later," she shouted and scooted into the back seat. "Thank you Mr. Harvey."

I twisted around to face her. "Barbara's going to the rink, too. And we're going riding Saturday. Can you go?"

Tamara face clouded and she shook her head. "I can't. My folks are both working. I have to babysit my brothers."

"Oh, too bad."

Every weekend Barbara and I hung out at the stables. When Tamara could make it and could afford to ride, she joined us. We became an adventurous, fun-loving, cowgirl trio. We lived, first for horseback riding, and second, for talking about boys.

CHAPTER ELEVEN
2015

Margaret and I sat swinging on the porch, enjoying the cool afternoon. It was one of those perfect eighty degree California days which made all the state's negatives worthwhile. I shared my memories of Barbara and me and our many horseback riding escapades as Margaet used her bare foot to dangle and nudge the swing gently back and forth.

"Thank goodness I had horseback riding with Barbara before my life fell apart," I said. "It was the best time of my life. You went riding too, didn't you? At those people's house down the street?"

Margaret grimaced and shrugged. "Yes, I did. They competed at rodeos and when they were out of town at a rodeo I took care of the horses that they didn't take with them. In payment, they allowed me to ride anytime I wanted. Their pasture was set up to practice barrel racing, so I raced around those barrels every time I went to feed."

"Really? I didn't know that. I'll bet that was fun."

She nodded. "It was, but they were stupid to let me do that. What if I had fallen off?"

"I guess you have a point. But doesn't the memory of racing around those barrels thrill you? Isn't it a happy memory?"

Margaret shook her head. "They were stupid and irresponsible to let me ride alone."

I tried to shake off Margaret's gloom. "Mom and Dad were the same way," I said. " And so were Barbara's parents. They never worried. It didn't matter where or how far we rode, or how long we were gone. 'Just be home by dark,' they'd say, as I headed out the door.

I turned sideways, facing Margaret and pulled my knees to my chest. "Every weekend I rushed to finish my grooming and chores. Whatever money I earned, I crammed in my pocket and met Barbara at the stables. I plopped down my stash, paying for as many hours of riding as my money would buy. Barbara and I rode over miles and miles of countryside, never returning until the stables closed or when my money ran out, whichever came first.

"It may have been stupid of them," I said. "But I'm glad they didn't care. It was wonderful. "

I gazed off for a moment, watching the trees sway in the breeze. I sent up a silent thank you to God or the universe — to whoever was responsible for my wonderful childhood. The freedom of those days gave me the strength for the days ahead.

"Do you remember when Dad was teaching you to drive?" I asked. " I wasn't old enough yet. I whined and cried until he let me go along. He took us out on the Old Mine Road for a lesson, remember?"

Margaret nodded. "You were such a crybaby. You whined every time you didn't get your way. It always worked on Dad." Margaret increased the sway of the swing.

"After you drove, Dad surprised me by announcing it was my turn. I was so excited." I remembered running around to the driver's side and climbing behind the wheel. "I felt so grown up. But he kept yelling at me, 'Let up the clutch! Give it some gas!' I forgot to steer." I laughed at the memory.

Margaret grinned. "I remember," she said. "We ended up in the ditch. The Jeep almost tipped over. Neighbors slowed as they drove by and asked him if he needed any help. I'll bet he was so embarrassed."

"He just climbed out, went around and kneeled down by front wheels. I remember thinking, 'What's he doing? Praying?' He wasn't a praying man. He switched the Jeep into four-wheel drive mode.

"'Get in the back seat.' That's all he said to me. Then he drove it out of the ditch." I laughed again.

"He never said a word all the way home. The poor man. If he only knew that was nothing compared to what I was going to put him through later."

Margaret forced a grin, which often came across as a smirk to me. Her serious nature was such a constant, like Dad. I wondered if she was afraid if she relaxed and let go, the gaiety would be snatched from her. But today I succeeded in hitting her funny bone, and it warmed me like it did when I amused Dad.

Margaret shook her finger at me. "Dad could never say no to you."

"Sometimes I could manipulate you, too." I said. "I was jealous when you began dating. Remember how I talked you and your boyfriend into fixing me up? We went on a double date.

"I sure do. You whined and bugged me 'til I fixed you up.

"The guys took us to the Old Mill Restaurant for dinner and then drove out to that abandoned farm. We sat on the bales of hay in front of that falling down barn and proceeded to get drunk."

Margaret swung gently. "You didn't know how to drink. I kept telling you to slow down."

"It was my first time. Lemonade and Sloe Gin. It tasted so good. I got so sick." I giggled.

"You got so drunk. I swore never again. I was afraid you would rat to Mom and Dad. You were such a tattle tale."

"I was, huh? Sorry about that. But that's how I got back at you, for teasing me."

Margaret only smirked again. She hadn't let that go either.

"You were always coming home from school crying," I said. "The kids at school always made fun of you and called you names."

Margaret hung her head. "Queenie. Everyone called me Queenie. I tried to hang out with you and Barbara but you always said no."

"I don't remember that."

"You had lots of friends." Margaret rose from the swing and walked out of the shade of the patio into the warm sunshine.

"You had lots of dates," I pointed out.

Margaret picked at a couple weeds, sprouting up through the decorative rock. "I had two dates before I started going steady."

"I only had two girlfriends."

Amused at our teenage perceptions, we both chuckled. "You, me, Mom and Dad. We all lived in our own little worlds," I said. "I took off to go horseback riding with Barbara every chance I could. You were always reading a book. And after Dad worked all day at the apartments and had dinner, he spent his evening in his bedroom, reading.

Once when I was home for the weekend from college, I asked Dad what had gone wrong with him and Mom. 'Your mother only had so much love to give,' he told me. "After you and your sister were born, she gave all her love to you girls.' He wasn't joking. He believed it. It was sad."

Margaret smirked. "Mom and Dad were not the smartest people. Dad didn't even graduate high school."

Again, that attitude. Queenie.

"But Dad was always studying. He never read novels, only non-fiction about religion and philosophy, as if he were searching for answers for himself. . Once he gave me a five volume set of books called, *The Teachings of the Life of the Masters of The Far East*."

"He gave me a set too." Margaret pinched off a leaf from the rosemary plant and smelled it. "He was excited about them and told me it was important to read them."

Did you?" I asked.

"No."

"Neither did I," I said. "How did we all we all live in that small house together and never know anything about each other? I've learned more about you since you have lived here in Sun City than the sixteen years when we shared a bedroom in Springfield."

"Me too," she said.

I extended my leg and poked her with my bare foot. "Like what?"

She thought a minute. "Like the friends you make, for one. I know you always made friends easily, but you have a girlfriend who graduated Harvard and another who's dating the Chief Administrator of the L. A. Police department. And I am amazed by how many people in town know you. Everytime we go anywhere we run into people who know you. This entire neighborhood knows you."

I flushed and shook my head. "It's not what you're thinking, really. Everyone knows me because I groom practically everyone's dog in this town.

"And I didn't know you were such a good cook," Margaret said. "The Thanksgiving turkey was wonderful. And Grandma's strudel, too. It was just like I remembered."

I raised my brows. " Thank you. I don't know why you're surprised. I didn't get this fat being a bad cook."

Margaret went on. "What surprises me most is your book career. I don't know how you can just jump in and start writing books all of a sudden. You just dive into something new and don't look back."

"Eighty per cent of the people have thought about writing a book." I said.

"Did you?" Margarret asked.

"No, I admit I wasn't ever one of them. I never planned to be a published author. I only took that creative writing class for fun."

I sat up straighter. "You're right. When I want to do something, I just do it." I shook my head, surprised at the revelation. "But that attitude got me in trouble, too."

I thought of Margaret's life. When she married Simon and lived in L.A. She ran in the social circles she'd dreamed of. Her huge home was one block from Michael Jackson's family home. Her children went to school with Michael Landon's children and other famous Hollywood stars. Margaret would never wear the same outfit twice to the theater, or a concert, or luncheon. Every Saturday, she attended temple with her husband and his family. The parties they threw were gracious, kosher and catered. She had fulfilled her childhood dream. I wondered if she had ever met Nicky Hilton or Liz Taylor.

On a death watch, you get to know someone. Margaret coddled her sons. Was it to make up for her husband's harsh and abusive behavior for which she never developed a backbone against — not even thirty years later after the divorce?

But we were raised to contain our anger, we both avoided confrontations. I'll admit I could be pushed to a boiling point, but never had I witnessed Margaret even raising her voice.Margaret never rocked the boat. She sold her serenity, for the price of the glittery L.A. lifestyle. When Simon became so blatant with his affairs she could no longer look the other way. She calmly divorced him.

No, I could never have played the lifetime role Margaret had. My devil-may-care, self-possessed attitude was as strong as hers was kindly and caring. Her dependent, don't hurt anyone's feeling disposition balanced on the opposite end of the scale against my independent do-not-need-anyone profile. Open throttle, full speed, was the only gear I knew. I couldn't imagine living any other way.

CHAPTER TWELVE
1964

At school, anytime Gary walked by, his gaze met mine and held until my face flushed and I looked away. Sometimes we brushed shoulders, and I braved a closer glance. His wide-set blue eyes squinted ever so slightly from the faintest of a grin which I doubted anyone noticed but me. A hint of amusement. A couple strands escaped his Pomade plastered hair, threatening to fall below his brow. Once when I thought he was far enough away not to notice, I spun around and studied his swagger, his 501 jeans and the bulge on his arm from the pack of Marlboros rolled up in his t-shirt sleeve. But he must have sensed my stare. He swiveled back around, walking backwards and shot a suggestive grin in my direction.

He didn't hang out with the football players or cheerleaders, I knew that. His buddy, Chris, attended Lanphier High, across town. And the girls hanging around Gary? I never saw them in the halls. Probably drop outs. They smoked. And the way they dressed and acted proved they liked to put out.

Everyone knew what their kind was like. They weren't smart and would end up getting pregnant and living on the east side with a bunch of screaming filthy kids and a drunk husband. Their home would be a shack with a yard full of weeds and a porch with broken slats. A couch with springs poking out of it would be on the front porch instead of a swing.

On the first day of my junior year, I trudged up the stairs to the low track English class tucked away in the far corner of the third floor. My poor grade the previous year landed me here in the nose bleed section of the building as if to separate us underachievers from the more honorable students.

I tugged open the heavy classroom door and glanced around the room. A middle aisle split the desks in the classroom. Gary's buddy, Larry, sat in the back row. No surprise. The first surprise came when I recognized John, the class president. He sat in the front row. His presence comforted me. Maybe I wasn't so stupid after all. I took a seat on the left side of the aisle right behind him.

No one talked. It was like that on the first day. My second surprise came when the door swooshed open and Gary strode in. He paused, too. Those eyes. They swept over me and around the room.

Larry called out. "You gonna stand there all day? Over here!" He pointed to the unoccupied desk beside him. Gary nodded at Larry, then gave me that crooked grin and took the seat directly across the aisle from me.

I focused on the front of the classroom but I knew he was looking at me. I ran my hand over the sleeve of my favorite blue angora sweater, glad I'd worn it. I crossed my legs and restrained my dangling foot from its rhythmical swinging. The heat of his gaze traveled up my bare leg and I flushed. Dropping my eyes, I studied my stack of books atop my desk and wondered if he could hear my heart pounding.

In the classroom, throughout the entire semester, we never spoke, but now when we passed in the halls, I said, "Hi."

He nodded. I think he smiled. But nothing more.

I hoped I appeared in control like him, but inside everything was happening. My heart pounded, I found it difficult to catch my breath, and I blushed because I sensed he knew his effect on me. His ghost-like smile only intensified the storm raging within me. I dreamed about him. I wrote his name next to mine, and I told Mom I loved him. Those days in that English class passed too quickly. I dreaded the last day when I would no longer see him.

Barbara thought Gary was cute enough, but for me, the more we talked about him, the more my infatuation grew. I lingered in the halls at school, waiting for him to pass, and I hung out near his locker. For Barbara's sixteenth birthday her parents gave her a brand-new, baby-blue Buick Special convertible. We no longer sat at home on Saturday nights. We cruised. Pulling into McDonald's with the top up, Barbara parked and depressed a button. The ragtop rose high, moved rearward, and folded up as it lowered and disappeared behind the back seat. While it folded away, we primped, brushing our hair and freshening our lipstick, confident everyone noticed.

We frequented all the hangouts, the Steak 'N Shake, Cozy Dog and Bob's Big Boy. Each time Barbara and I saw Gary, we laughed and giggled. If he noticed us, he shot me the slightest nod and grin, almost unnoticeable, but enough to send shivers right through me. I dreamed he would ask me out.

My junior year sped on. Margaret and I spent the weekends grooming dogs and mowing the grass at home, as well as the lawn of the house next door, of which Margaret and I were now owners, but I still made time for horseback riding and cruising the hangouts with Barbara.

Dad found an old Pontiac for me. It was sound running, not pretty like Barbara's car, but I was happy to have it. I paid for it from my savings. "Always keep two quarts of oil in the trunk," Dad said. "If the gas station attendant says your car is low on oil, give him one of the cans."

I was turning sixteen, owned a car and, except for that English class, I made A's and B's. Life was easy. Studying was a cinch for me but not so for Margaret. She froze up on test days and came home with C's and D's even though she studied. She had one girlfriend. The other kids made fun of her. I think they did because she had an air about her, like she was too good for them, the school and even the town. She asked several times to hang out with me and my friends, but I wanted no more of Margaret's big sister bossiness. Her years of teasing had taken their toll on our relationship. And I was done with being called stupid and being treated like I was dumb. I wanted to be on my own.

Yet, I envied Margaret. She had a boyfriend. I'd only had that double date which she had arranged.

On the last day of class, before summer vacation arrived the thought struck me that after today I would not see Gary until September.

Every day, when the bell rang, Gary burst out of the classroom, reaching the hall before me, and sprinted down the three flights of stairs, where he pushed out the back door exit with just enough time to grab a cigarette before his next class.

Today when the bell rang, he grasped his pen so tightly, it snapped in two. Clutching his books, he scrambled from his desk, tossed the pen in the trash, and rushed out of the classroom. A cloud of sadness slowed my gait as I exited the classroom and watched his retreat toward the stairs. But at the top of the steps he paused and turned back as the rest of the students drained into the hall.

He scanned the crowd before he threw another glance back toward the stairs, as if looking for someone. As I approached, he spun around. startled, and pulled up short.

He stood there, face to face each of us squeezing our books to our chests. Any closer, our arms would have touched. I smelled his cologne. My throat tightened.

"Sorry," he said.

I wondered why he apologized. I smiled.

He dropped his arms, as if to hold his books low in front of him, but they slipped from his grip and tumbled to the floor. As he squatted, I stepped around him to leave.

"Wait," he said. I turned back. His panicked face peered up at me as he fumbled to gather his books "Please, wait."

I knelt down in front of him. He glanced up my skirt but jerked his gaze away, then coughed and sort of choked. I reached for his English book, and his hand touched mine. We both jerked back as if we had been burned.

"Sorry," he said one more time.

I rose up and he, too, shot upright. Reaching out, I handed him the book. As he grabbed it, I said, "Have a great summer."

He stood in place as I walked away. I had progressed halfway down the first flight of stairs when I heard him shout.

"Wait!" The rest of the class stampeded down the stairs behind me, the clatter muffling his words. "Janice, wait up!"

My breath caught, surprised to see him, again, so close beside me.

The corners of his eyes crinkled, his mouth straight-lined. "You have a great summer, too," he said, and shoved past me, rattling down the next flight. His boots echoed in the stairwell, drowning out the thundering herd of students milling past me. He reached the second landing, clung to the worn oak bannister a moment, as if out of breath, then strode to the drinking fountain and gulped the water from the spout.

When I reached the landing, I came up behind him, where he hunched over, gripping the edges of the water fountain. "Are you okay?" I asked.

He spun around. "I was wondering if you would like to go out tomorrow night?"

His words sounded faraway, like in one of my dreams. Had he just asked me out? Time stretched out like those seconds before a baseball connects with the bat.

I gazed into those eyes. His eyebrows raised. A muscle twitched in his neck. He *was* asking me out.
"Sure." I said. The word cracked loud through the air. That's all I could say. He broke into a sheepish smile. Yes! He *had* asked me out! I turned and started to leave, embarrassed because I didn't know what else to say. A light shock went through me when I felt his touch on my shoulder, pulling me back to face him.
"Sure?" he said." Do you mean yes?"
I didn't recognize my own voice. "Yes. I said yes."
"I'll pick you up at seven." He blurted out the words, swung around and clambered down the last flight of stairs. Shoving through the heavy fire exit door, he disappeared into the alley. The door swooshed close.

CHAPTER THIRTEEN
2015

The hospice nurse folded up the stethoscope and stuffed it in her pocket. "Since you've been feeling some discomfort, I talked to the doctor. He's going to increase your pain meds. They'll be delivering the new prescription before eight tonight. Do you have any questions?"

Margaret frowned. "I don't think you need to increase the dosage. I told you I just think I over did it the other day with everyone visiting."

"That's okay. You don't have to take them if you don't want to. You still have a few days' supply of the lower dosage that you're now taking. But I advise you to take the increased dose. If you let the pain get too intense, it becomes difficult to control. I don't want you to be uncomfortable." She checked her clipboard. "Dr. Mesa came by yesterday didn't he? "

Margaret tilted her head and raised her brow and frowned. "Yes, he did. He was here for an entire ten minutes."

The nurse smiled. "I know he's pretty abrupt. That's the biggest complaint we get about him."

Margaret smirked. "I'm from L.A. At Cedars Sinai I've been treated by the best doctors in the country. My cancer doctor was the President's doctor."

"I'm sorry. Dr. Mesa …."

"Not just a CEO President. THE President."

The nurse pressed her lips together and nodded.

"Even though the doctors at Cedars are very busy with such important people, they always took the time to be polite and thorough with me. I expected the same treatment from Dr. Mesa, but was very disappointed. I have never been treated with such ineptitude and abruptness."

I stood at the foot of the bed, wishing I could crawl under it. Heat from my embarrassment warmed my face. I was sure the nurse dealt with many difficult patients. I only hoped she knew I didn't hold the same elitist attitude, which my sister now revealed.

The woman waited a moment to be sure Margaret finished and then tried again. "I'm sorry. Let me see if I can get Dr. Feinstein. I'll check his schedule. I'm am sure you'll like him."

I restrained a smile. The nurse knew how to calm a situation.

"Thank you," Margaret said. "I don't want to deal with Mesa again."

The nurse stuffed her paperwork into her bag. "Any other questions? Concerns?" She gathered up her appointment book and clipboard. "I'm just going to step out in the living room and text Dr. Feinstein to get his schedule and I will call in the new prescription to the pharmacy. I'll be right back."

Margaret tthat

raised her chin in regal victory, her lips forming a narrow line. Margaret motioned for me to come closer. I leaned in. "I'll talk to Michael when he comes tomorrow. I don't trust the medication changes. I need his opinion."

Margaret constantly questioned the competency of the doctors and nurses. She never asked my opinion. I pushed down my irritation but must not have restrained a smirk.

"The doctors and nurses in L.A. are better trained."

"Really?" I spit out the word sharply. "We can't have good health care way out here in the Inland Empire?"

"Oh, of course you can, dear. I'm sure some have moved from L.A. out to this area like I have."

And there it was. I was the red-neck little sister, the bad seed, the one without a degree.

"Would you go to the store for me? I need a few things for dinner tomorrow. Everyone will be here about noon.

"Sure," I said.

Thanksgiving dinner was pre-ordered, which is something Margaret never had done before, but in her condition she would be pushing herself to the limit to organize and entertain all day. The visit would exhaust her.

Daniel sat across the table from me, his two children sitting between him and his wife. Eleven-year old Ariel, sat straight backed and proper in her chair. Next to her, sat her three-year old brother, Danny Jr., a younger version of his sister. Both had the raven hair of their Japanese mother.

As Daniel dished up the mashed potatoes,

 To his children, I glanced at Margaret at the head of the table. "Everything looks really good," I said to her. "I can't wait to taste the salad, you always make a great salad."

Michael and Tonya's two-year old, Benny, sat between them, banging his fist on the high chair tray. Both parents focused on feeding him yams. "Here comes the airplane." Michael announced in a silly voice, maneuvering a spoonful through a figure eight pattern and hopefully into the child's open mouth. Tonya waited, napkin poised, to wipe the boy's mouth.

As the contents neared the boy's mouth, the child squished up his face, swung his head sideways and cried. Michael's grin distorted. "Come on, Munchkin. If you don't finish your Thanksgiving dinner, there will be no pumpkin pie for you." The toddler banged his fist on the tray and screeched again. "You want pie, don't you? It's your favorite." Michael's voiced whined.

Benny shook his head sharply. "No!"

Tonya laid her hand on the boy's forehead. "He's warm. He's probably coming down with something, again."

"He's always getting sick since he started day care," Daniel said.

"You're still on the waiting list for Disney's Day Care?" Margaret asked.

"Yes. It'll be another five weeks. I can't wait to get him out of this private one." Michael stabbed at the platter of sliced turkey. "Mexicans aren't the cleanest people. That's why he's always getting sick."

I looked up. What? I scanned the faces before me. As Daniel slathered butter on his roll, he nodded in response.

Intent on their dinners, everyone grunted in agreement. Denise, Daniel, even Simon and his new wife. The tinging of the fine silver and clinking of the crystal glassware resounded in my ears. Margaret perched like a queen on her throne in a storybook, unfazed by the comment. Her too? Who was this woman?

Mom and Dad did not raise us that way. "The colored are just like us," Mom and Dad would say. But now looking back, did they believe that? When prospective black tenants inquired about an empty apartment, they asked, "Do you rent to blacks?" If Margaret or I took the call we were instructed to answer, "There are a lot of white people we don't rent to."

My grandmother hid blacks in her basement for the Underground Railroad. But to buck society publicly? That did not happen at our house.

But now? This day and age? Did they talk freely, because my opinions were of no concern? Or did they believe my views were in line with theirs? I felt creeped out. I couldn't wait for this day of thankfulness to be over.

"I helped make the salad," Ariel said as she stirred and poked at the food on her plate. Her proud, child-like smile spread across her youthful face, which had begun to lose its roundness. The hint of puberty promised an alluring symmetry. She looked at me. "I washed the lettuce and the tomatoes."

Daniel leaned in close to the child as if to whisper but did not lower his voice. "That's fine, but if you don't quit playing with your food you're going to get a timeout."

Ariel's dark eyes swept the table. Her prideful smile turned crooked. If Daniel recognized her embarrassment, he didn't react, or maybe he didn't care. Could it have been his intention? Her gaze landed back on me before she dropped her head and hovered over her plate. I wanted to hug her.

"When your Grandma Margaret and I were your age we used to sneak out at night into the neighbors' gardens with a salt shaker. We stole tomatoes right off the vine and ate them. We never washed them."

Ariel's eyes widened, again searching for the family's reaction. There was none. Stealing and eating unwashed tomatoes appeared to be a concept too difficult for her to grasp.

Ariel peered down the table at her grandmother. "Is that true, Grandma? Why?"

Margaret sent a weak smile to everyone and would have flushed if she were not so pale.

I rescued her. "Oh, I don't know." I said. "Because we didn't have a garden. Because we weren't supposed to. Because it was fun. The point was that we ate tomatoes, raspberries and blackberries right off the bushes and picked the cherries right off the trees without washing them."

Tight lipped, Daniel pushed back in his chair. "Yes, but back then they didn't spray everything with chemicals."

"I beg to differ," I said as I shot his a smug smile. "DDT was used on all the crops. That's how all the creeks and rivers in the Midwest became polluted." I felt a tingle of victory over the man with a PhD in political science.

CHAPTER FOURTEEN
1964

Gary's fifty-seven Chevy sputtered up the drive. I stepped up to my bedroom window and peeked through the part in the curtains. He had washed his car. It was always clean but the hood caught the streetlight like moon rays on the lake. He climbed out of the car and approached the front door that we never used. His jeans drew a crease line down his pant legs, accenting his height. I clutched the bedroom curtain. His polished biker boots reflected the yellow glow of the porch light.

Romantic thoughts had raced around in my brain all day. Would he kiss me good night? Would he put his arm around me at the movie? Would he kiss me? I stepped away from the window. Pacing, I rehearsed what I might say to him and worried Mom and Dad would say to him.

The doorbell rang. I jumped. My heart pounded. I wrung my sweaty hands. I didn't know what to do. What should I talk about? Lucille Ball's voice and the audience laughter from the TV tittered under my closed bedroom door.

All day I fantasized about this night. I worried Dad would read my mind. What would he say to Gary? I grabbed one more look in the mirror. My lashes were heavy with mascara. The sight of my gold locket disappearing into my cleavage gave me a rush. I pulled it out, took a deep breath and jerked open the bedroom door.

Facing Dad, Gary stood like a Paul Bunyan in our small living room. For a moment pride flooded over my nervousness.

Gary looked my father in the eye, reached out his hand. "It's a pleasure to meet you, Sir," he said.

Dad shook his hand and stepped aside. "Come in. Janice will be right out."

The men both turned to me as I stepped into the living room. The room felt close. I moved to the side and flattened my back against the wall.

Gary smiled a real smile. Was it for the benefit of my father? "Hi, Janice. Are you ready to go?"

Mom hustled into the crowded room, wiping her hands on a dishtowel. Her ruffled apron couldn't hide her thick waist. Her hair was tousled. Why hadn't she combed her hair? I shot Gary a nervous smile as Mom greeted him. "How are you?" She said. "Janice says you're going to the movies. Which one?"

My stomach lurched. I cursed under my breath. They were being so nosey. I could tell Gary was stumped by the question. He drug his palms across his jeans, took a step closer to Mom and said, "It's nice to meet you, Mrs. Harvey."

"Janice has been dying to see, *Tammy and the Bachelor*." Mom said. She pointed to a straight chair. "Would you like to sit down?"

"No thank you, ma'am," Gary shoved his hands into his pockets and, shifting his weight, he glanced at the TV screen. Lucy was making one of her pouty faces at Ricky.

I took a deep breath and stepped away from the wall. "Hi, Gary." I said. I shot a look at my father, and then back at Gary who finally gave me that grin, the one I hoped Dad didn't notice. That something stirred in me, again. That something I'd felt before, only now it was even stronger. The gesture seemed so intimate here in my own living room.

I glanced at Dad. His eyes cold, his face hard like stone, fixed on Gary. He noticed.

I don't recall how we escaped. Gary opened the car door and I slid into the passenger seat. I glanced up at the living room picture window. Dad watched in the shadows behind the glass, I wanted to bolt, crawl in bed and pull the covers over my head. But I was excited too. I couldn't believe this was happening. I wiped my sweaty hands on my dress as Gary walked around the front of the car and got in.

He turned the ignition, the engine fired and rumbled. I was grateful for the DJ's voice on the radio as he shifted into reverse, and backed out of the drive. Gunning the accelerator, he sped away, hoping like me, I'm sure, that we could leave my father's image behind.

"I thought we would go to the drive-in," he said as he eased up to a stop sign. "Blue Hawaii is playing."

I loosened my grip on my dress bunched in my fist. "Sure. That would be nice."

We cruised Bob's Big Boy. As he eased through the parking lot, I pointed to a blue, Buick convertible. "There's my friend, Barbara."

I sat a little straighter and rolled down the window. Gary honked as I called out. "Hey Barb." She waved as Gary parked a few spaces down. He had *barely* flashed his headlights for service when the carhop arrived.

Chomping on gum, she Peering into the interior, she leaned down and peered into the interior. Giving me a catty smile, she said, "Hi Gary. What can I get ya?"

"Two cokes,"Gary glanced over at me. "Did you want some fries, too?"

"Do you?" I asked.

He turned back to the carhop. "An order of fries, too." The girl shot him a grin and he watched her pleated skirt brush the middle of her thighs as she sauntered down the row of hotrods and roadsters. She stopped at his buddy's Mustang. Larry leaned against the GTO's fender, his arm hooked around his girlfriend, Carla's waist. I may have been innocent but I didn't have to guess what Larry's plan for Carla would be at the Drive-in. Watching the movie was not part of it.

It didn't take long after the carhop brought our order for us to finish. Gary signaled the girl to pick up our tray by flashing his headlights and we were soon heading for the Drive-In.

"I've only been to the drive-in with my parents," I said.

"My parents used to take my sister and me, too," he said. "They always parked in the first two front rows, did yours?"

I nodded. "The playground was right there between the big screen and where we parked so they could keep an eye on us."

Gary lit a cigarette and blew the smoke out the window. "Before the movie my sister and I spent all our energies on the swing sets and teeter-totters."

"Our parents knew what they were doing." I grinned. "Maggie and I always fell asleep soon after the movie started, leaving them to watch the in peace."

"My sis and I did the same. I doubt if we ever watched a movie til the end." He said.

"If you're cool and have a date, you park in the last few rows." He said as he eased past the lines speakers mounted on posts and pulled up to one in the second to last row. Killing the engine, he turned off the headlights. It was dusk, nearly dark.

Removing the speaker from its pedestal, he hung it on the car's window and turned to me. Patting the the seat on the empty space next to him, he smiled his killer smile at me. I blinked. I felt my face blush and I slid over beside him. He put his arm around me, and pulled me close. I couldn't think of anything to say so I didn't say anything. I was sure he could hear my heart pounding,

Bang!

I jumped at the loud thump that sounded from the back of the car just as Gary's buddy, Larry, slammed his palm on the trunk lid and then popped his head halfway into the passenger side window. A devilish grin spread across his buddy's face. "Hey!" he said. He rested his arms on the open window ledge, a beer in one hand and cigarette in the other. "Aren't you going to introduce me?" He smiled, never taking his eyes off me and took a drag from his cigarette. His beer breath floated across the seat on the puff of smoke.

"No, I'm not. She's a good girl. "

Larry scoffed and took a long swig from his beer. "You're no fun." He straightened and turned back to join his buddies. "Come by at intermission. Me and Carla, we've got cold beer."

"Not tonight."

Larry paused. He bent down again. Peering back inside, he said, "I get it, Bud." He flashed a big grin at me. "I don't blame you for wanting to keep her to yourself." He held up his bottle as if in a toast. I scooted even closer to Gary.

I tried to get into the movie. My hair draped over his arm. I had washed it with shampoo that smelled like lilacs. I couldn't concentrate. He touched a lock of my hair and twisted it around his finger. I gazed up at him, his lips so close to mine I couldn't breathe. I could hear my heart thumping. He withdrew his arm from my shoulder and fumbled for a cigarette.

When he took me home, we stood beneath the back porch light and I told him what a nice time it had been. He kissed me lightly on the lips. I was grateful for my practice time with Barbara.

"I had a great time too," he said.

I didn't know what to say or do so I yanked open the screen door. I couldn't get inside fast enough.

CHAPTER FIFTEEN
2015

"Do you remember how we spent every weekend grooming dogs?" I asked. "We sang to 50'S tunes and groomed about what — ten dogs each day? At five dollars per dog, that was good money for kids our age." I said.

Margaret smiled at the memory. "Did you ever wonder why we worked like that without ever complaining? How did Mom get us to do that?"

"I've wondered, too," I said. "Times were different. Parents expected more and kids did what was expected of them,"

Margaret was in a talkative mood. "Remember when we turned fifteen and sixteen? She arranged that we buy Harry's house next-door when he moved his family to California?"

I laughed. "After that not only did we do all that grooming, but we also had to cut the grass and do chores for that house, too."

"Mom sold the property when I went to college," Margaret said.

I stuffed the folded sweats into a drawer. "Remember how she wrote to that teen magazine, Seventeen?"

"I remember." The tone in Margaret's voice caused me to turn, catching the smirk on her face. *Was that disdain?*

"You sure ruined that," she said.

Yep, it was a tone. Was she still angry about that?

I shrugged off her attitude and chuckled. "I did, didn't I? We all had our dreams about that. The magazine was going to publish our story — *Two enterprising teenage girls running their own business.*" I swirled around in the room as if doing a pirouette. "You were going to go to Disneyland and become a Mouseketeer in the Mickey Mouse Club. That article was going to be your ticket out of Springfield. You had Hollywood stars in your eyes."

Margaret shot me a crooked grin. "Mom figured she'd earned bragging rights, after all the time she had invested in us."

The dryer buzzed. I leaned down and kissed Margaret's forehead. "I'm sorry I ruined your chance to become a Mouseketeer."

In the garage, I pulled the warm clothing from the dryer as I revisited the lost opportunity. I found it all quite amusing.

No, the plane carrying the magazine team didn't crash, John F Kennedy hadn't been assassinated yet, and I didn't break out with hives or a bad case of acne. What was the life changer?

Before the New York magazine's photo team was scheduled to swoop into our little town and lift us away to stardom … I got pregnant.

Mom felt compelled to confess my wayward ways to the magazine and they cancelled the event. A story about an "easy" sixteen year old who had no morals would not sell, no matter what the girl had accomplished.

Back in the bedroom, I yanked a blouse from the laundry basket and shook it a little too harshly. Pangs of past embarrassment and contempt tore at me, still. I smirked back in disdain.

"By the way," I said as I slipped the blouse onto a hanger. "Ashley suggested that maybe Charlotte might want to see you. What do you think? Should I try to find her? Do you want to see her?"

Margaret turned and gazed out the window. "No, please don't." She sighed and hung her head. "I always felt I failed her."

I laid down the shorts I had been folding and looked at her, surprised by her statement. Charlotte was fifteen years old when I sent her to live with Margaret. I had no control her. I couldn't even get her to go to school. "Really? I said. "I never thought that. At least you and Simon got her to graduate. I couldn't even get her to go to school."

Margaret massaged her neck as if uneasy with the subject.

"Anyway," I said. "It's been sixteen years. If she were clean and sober I'm sure I would have heard from her." My voice cracked. "Her oldest daughter, Jasmine, was eleven when I saw them last.She looked just like Charlotte when she was that age."

"Jasmine's little sister, Julia, was a blonde cutie. Nate suggested that maybe they would try to contact me when they grew up." Sixteen years was such a long time, I thought. "She's not on Facebook. I've looked. I figure she's probably dead or brain dead."

I chewed my lip and ran my fingers through my hair. Every time I visited the subject of Charlotte, gnawing guilt ate at me. This was how loneliness was going to feel with Margaret gone.

Nate's granddaughter, Celia, and her family told me all the time I was family but I figured they felt obligated because I had been married to her grandfather. I couldn't imagine how they could feel that way. weren't blood.

I shoved the problem away. Smoothing the pile of folded laundry on my lap, I said, "I never really thanked you for taking Charlotte in. It meant so much to me." I turned from her and squeezed my eyes shut, pushing back age old tears. "I had felt like such a failure. I'll never forget what you said to me that day to make me feel better."

"What was that?"

"You said I was so young, and that I had done the best I could. "'Raising kids is hard,' you had said, even for you. You told me you couldn't have done it without Simon's help. You told me that you couldn't imagine how anyone could do it alone." I swiped at the tears streaming down my cheeks. Leaning in, I kissed Margaret. "You made me feel so much better that day."

"We all do the best we can." Margaret didn't embellish. She cleared her throat and fiddled with the bed covers. She made it obvious she didn't want to talk more about the subject.

I shrugged, dismissing her silence, and waved my hand over her sickbed. "Later, after all this is done, i'm going to find her. Even if she hasn't straightened out. I have so much to say to her. I don't care if I did do the best I could. She needs to know how sorry I am for my mistakes. I want her to know I'm aware of my damaging behavior, of how unsupportive I was. I don't care if she's drunk or wasted, or clean and sober. I need her to know how sorry I am."

Margaret started to say something. I raised my palm to silence her. "I know. I know," I said. "I did the best I could. I believe that. But I'm not going to hide behind it either. I want her to know I own my part in it. She needs to know."

Margaret rubbed the back of her hands and hugged her own shoulders. "I still feel I failed her," she said.

I didn't know why Margaret clung to her guilt, but I carried enough of my own. I tasted the bile boil in my throat as the disgusting night when I lost my virginity replayed it's ugly scene in my head.

CHAPTER SIXTEEN

1964

Washed out red curls hung in his eyes and matched the freckles clustered thick on his short arms. His short legs made him appear stocky under his baggy jeans, which draped over his roller skates. He rolled back and forth on his heels in place as his eyes scanned me up and down. I ignored that my skin prickled. "Would you like to skate, again?"

No boy had ever asked me to skate and now he was asking me, again. "Sure." I grinned sheepishly at Barbara as he grabbed my hand and pulled me into the crowd skating by. Glancing back, I hollered to Barbara, "Later."

He probably asked my name, but I was too nervous to remember. His was Randy. His sweaty hand clutched mine as we skated a few rounds until intermission. When we glided past the couples on the floor I smiled at them as if I were now one of them.

The music stopped and we skated off the polished wood floor with all the others as I noticed Gary leaving the building. I hated it when he wasn't at the rink, even though he didn't skate or pay any attention to me, he always had his eyes on me. I fantasied that I was the only one Gary watched as Randy led me to an uncrowded corner of the rink and asked, "Would you like something to drink?"

"I guess so."

He swiveled around, and then spun back, facing me, showing off his expertise on the skates. He nodded toward the lines at the snack bar and frowned. "Look at the lines. Why don't we go out to my car? I have something to drink there. We can listen to the radio."

"Okay." Wow. I was going out to his car. We removed our skates and put on our street shoes and coats. As we headed for the door, I scanned the crowd, looking for Gary, but didn't see him. His car wasn't in the parking lot either.

At Randy's car he laughed at the couple sitting in his front seat. "Looks like my buddy had the same Idea. We'll sit in the back."

I scooted in and he climbed in next to me, pulling me close beside him. "Hey, pour us some of that," Randy said to his friend who held a thermos.

His buddy handed over two Styrofoam cups and said, "You owe me."

I took a sip and was relieved it wasn't Sloe Gin. Randy's friend and his girl ignored us and began making out. She giggled and disappeared as she lay down on the front seat. Randy's buddy flopped on top of her.

Randy tossed my empty cup to the floorboard and started kissing me. Gary's image flashed in my mind, and then my father's. Randy was breathing like a bull. His hand pushed up my blouse and his fingers crawled under my bra. He rubbed my breasts and a warmth flushed over me. Now his hand wormed under my skirt's waistband. "Just lean back," he said.

I lay down on the seat like the girl in the front. Blood pounded in my head. His fingers worked a magic that I didn't want to stop. Now, on top of me, his weight made it hard to breathe. He pressed his mouth hard against mine. His fingers moved inside me and an unfamiliar rush followed. A surprising spasm pulsed through me and my body tickling and tingling with an intense pleasurable ache. Before the sensation died, he climbed off of me, zipped up his jeans and said, "Come on. Let's go back inside."

My head still spun and my mind fumbled with what had happened.

The next morning I woke up late and stretched, enjoying the warmth of my bed. A soreness between my legs reminded me of last night. I wasn't sure what had happened, but by the time I arrived home, I had a creepy feeling, and a voice pounding in my head complained, wishing whatever it was, hadn't happened. I showered, letting the hot water drown out the chatter.

Last night's overwhelming sensations sprang into my thoughts, and despite the soreness, my body reacted. As I recalled last night's throbbing surges, heat flushed my face. And again, my heartbeat quickened. I thought of Gary. His kisses stirred reactions in me, too, but not the quaking rush like I had felt last night. And never the uncomfortable feelings of shame and wrongness, which I now felt. I shook off the confusion and padded to the bathroom.

Returning to my room, Mom stood, lock-kneed, like a sentry at my door. Her mouth drew a solemn line but failed to hold in the bitterness from her eyes. Startled, my forehead raised in question. "What's wrong?" I asked.

She raised her arm, waving a pair of my panties in my face. "This! This is what's wrong!" Her face twisted, baring her teeth and causing her to squint. Tears leaked from the corners of her eyes. She held my panties from last night, the ones I had tossed in the clothes hamper.

Not understanding why, my cheeks burned hot. Guilt flooded over me. The last remnants of sensual memories dissipated, not only of last night, but also the sweet ones of Gary.

Mom pointed to the bloody spot staining the crotch of my underpants. "Were you with Gary last night?" I didn't know what she was talking about, but her fiery attitude frightened me.

"I was with Randy," I said.

And then it all made sense to me.

A snowstorm raged dark and silent outside. I sat on the couch, Mom and Dad flanking me. I couldn't believe this was happening. The rabbit had died. At first I didn't know what that meant. It meant the pregnancy test was positive, I was going to have a baby. The shock of my situation reverberated throughout the little house without a sound.

Momma said there would be days like this. Momma said .... The muffled music of the Shirellles from Margaret's transistor radio drifted out from under our closed bedroom door.

Dad sat to my left. His shoulders slumped and his slackened jowls made his face appear longer than it was. I wondered how old he was. "You have three options," he began. "You could get married."

I started to say I don't even know the guy, I don't love him, I don't want to get married, but he raised his hand, silencing me.

"Getting married and keeping the baby will change your life forever."

His voice was gruff and gravelly. I thought he was going to cry.

"Or, you could go away, have the baby and put it up for adoption."

"Go away?" He had my attention now. I didn't want to go away. I looked up at him.

Avoiding my questioning look, his eyes dropped to his lap. He wiped his hands on his trousers and then met Mom's worried look.

"Or, you could get an abortion."

Mom gasped. She could not look at me either. She dabbed at her tears with a balled-up tissue. Mom didn't explain why she cried, or the fear in her eyes. Dad didn't say why he wanted to send me away. The blizzard howled outside while the snow swirled and danced in colorful patterns under the streetlight. .

I didn't explain my decision either.

"I've already talked to Randy. We're going to get married."

And then Dad did cry.

CHAPTER SEVENTEEN
2015

I dumped the last load of clothes, still warm from the dryer onto the foot of the bed. "How were you so lucky as to not get pregnant? You dated Bob all through high school," I asked.

"I never slept with him." Margaret said. "We made out a lot, but that's all. And at college, Stanley and I got married first, and after that I took the pill."

"What? You believed in 'no sex until you're married'? Really?"

Margaret raised her brow and tilted her head as if surprised anyone would believe differently.

"After I divorced Charlotte's father, Gary and I started dating again. He would drive the ninety miles to

Champaign to see me. He always made sure we were careful. I tried to get the pill, but you had to be married before the doctors would prescribe it."

Margaret raised her brow again. "Really? I didn't know that."

"That's the way it was then. Women weren't supposed to have sex out of wedlock. Period." I grinned at Margaret. "Good girls like you didn't need to know that fact."

Margaret tilted her head and sent me a doubtful look concerning my "good girl" statement.

"Word around campus was that there was a doctor who ignored the law, but it ended up I didn't have to seek him out. I developed female issues, which caused excessive bleeding. I became so anemic the university doctor hospitalized me, gave me two pints of blood and prescribed the pill to control my heavy periods."

Margaret's face softened. "I didn't know that you went through all that either."

"I was relieved. I didn't want another baby. I didn't even know how to take care of Charlotte.

"I was at a loss in the parenting department, too," Margaret said. "I was not the nurturing kind. When I had the boys, Simon's mom and his sister were a great help."

"Do you remember when we used to baby sit the kids next door?" I asked.

"Only once or twice from what I remember. I hated babysitting," Margaret said. "Neither one of us knew what to do. We never even played with dolls."

"When Charlotte cried I could never figure out what was wrong or what she wanted. At college, I enrolled her in the university daycare, but I often left her in Springfield with Mom and Dad and only saw her on weekends when I drove home to groom dogs.

"And boy did Mom and Dad spoil her." I said. "They weren't like when we grew up. They allowed her to jump on the bed. She didn't have to eat her vegetables. Dad took her to the park all the time and Mom bought her clothes — new clothes. No Salvation Army clothes for Charlotte. I was immature enough to be jealous."

Charlotte was five when her grandfather passed away and then her grandmother passed four years later. What a loss it must have been for her, I thought now. She received no comfort from me, but by then I'm sure Charlotte had learned not to expect any emotional support from me, just as I had learned the same from my parents by that age. Feelings were a taboo subject. By the time Charlotte turned sixteen her perfect grades had begun to fall.

"I had been a single parent for some time. I was either working or going out with friends, so Charlotte was pretty much on her own. Her drinking problem developed right under my clueless nose. Her grades dropped and her attitude rose out of control. Fifteen years of my neglectful parenting and lack of understanding had taken its toll on my Charlotte's sweet soul. Involved in my own immature and self-seeking journey, I never saw it coming."

"One day she was the sweetest little girl, and then overnight, she bucked me at every turn. Do you remember what you told me once when she was about eleven?"

Margaret smiled. "No what?"

"You only wished Michael and Daniel would turn out as well."

Margaret and I shook our heads at the irony. Shaking out a sweatshirt still warm from the dryer, I smoothed it out on the bed and folded it. I leaned back in my chair, stared out the window, lost in my story telling.

"She acted out. I responded. We no longer sang our favorite Helen Reddy song, *You And Me Against The World.* She had followed in my stubborn, know-it-all footsteps. I refused to admit my mistakes as a mother and Charlotte denied her addiction. The hurt and anger grew between us until we hated each other."

I placed the clothes carefully in the dresser drawer as I reviewed the path which led to the loss of my daughter. My fortress of delusional pride and confidence no longer worked for me. The stronghold came crumbling down. My life shattered.

"I rushed to shrinks and 12 step programs to repair my damaged ego. I wanted my sweet daughter back on track. A counselor mentioned I might have to change my stubborn attitude. I disagreed.

My voice cracked as I relived the memory. "I had found a stack of absentee notices from the school under Charlotte's mattress. We had a big argument. In a last-ditch effort, I showed Charlotte who was in control. I kicked her out. And like a normal, rebellious, over-confident fifteen-year -old would react, she stomped out the door, hurt and angry."

"I remember you calling me, and crying," Margaret said. "You were in a panic. You told me, 'I can't handle her. She keeps ditching school. I asked you what're you going to do? You told me you had already called the cops."

I fought back tears that always threatened when I relived the scenes in my mind. "The cops told me they would talk to Charlotte, but that was all they could do. The officer explained to Charlotte that she couldn't stay at her friends forever and sooner or later the parents would ask her to leave. 'Where will you go?' He asked. 'You won't have any money and you're too young to get a job. Then you'll have to steal. So sooner or later you will end up in Juvie. So why don't you just come with me now?' "

My fifteen-year-old baby girl was on the fast track for a foster home. Something had gone terribly wrong and I didn't even know why. All I knew was that I had failed terribly as a mother.

"That's when I told you I would take her in.," Margaret said.

I choked, remembering the emotional relief I had felt. My sweet, sweet caring Maggie had come to my rescue.

I had grasped ahold of Margaret's offer as if it were a drink of water and I were a stranded traveler wandering the desert. Margaret would attempt to repair the damage I had done.

With Charlotte living with Margaret, I spent my time nurturing my guilt and feeding it raw chunks of self-contempt. My depression grew like the appetite of a ravenous wild animal.

I considered suicide, but didn't know how many pills it would take to do the job. The idea of failing at the simple task of suicide would be the failure of all failures and would be more than I could bear, so I continued to endure my miserable life. I dragged my sorry self to 12 -step meetings. Very slowly and miraculously the program began to reveal the secrets of surviving in a world I had never understood. As the people in the meetings shared their stories, many so similar to mine, they explained how they had worked the steps. I began to gain the simple wisdom of the program. I learned to handle situations that used to baffle me."

I set the basket of folded clothes aside, and leaning back, I patted Margaret's leg. "You may not have known what to do as a mother, but you did all right with Daniel and Michael. They've turned out to be good boys. You should be proud."

Margaret fiddled with her Mother's birthstone necklace dangling loose over her breastbone. "I guess so."

"At least you got Charlotte to graduate high school," I said. "She may have given us all us the finger and took off on her own when she turned eighteen, but she did it with a high school diploma."

Shifting her weight, Margaret sat up straighter. "I was not perfect," she said. "When I would ask Michael to do his chores, he threw a fit and slammed things around. He knew his tantrums bothered me and that I would take the easy way out. I backed down and then told Daniel to do the chore instead. Michael would get out of his chores and Daniel was mad. I'm sure that's the root of Daniel's anger issues today."

I wondered if my nephews had resented Charlotte's coming to live with them. After returning the laundry basket to the garage, I took the dirty dishes to the kitchen and brought back a fresh glass of water. "Like you said, we all do the best we can. It applies to you too."

I thought it sad Margaret had come to no resolutions concerning her life. She had no belief in a higher power, she believed she had failed my daughter, and although she wouldn't admit it I sensed she was afraid of dying.

CHAPTER EIGHTEEN
2015

"Make sure you go through the freezer today," Margaret said. "Michael's coming tomorrow and Daniel's in town for Easter break. So Dad will be here too."

During every visit Michael inspected her refrigerator, searched for foods, which had passed their expiration dates and tossed them out. And then, marching to the store, he purchased updated, healthier, frozen dinners.

"I know. You don't want him to think you're not eating enough." I smiled. Did she really think Michael would believe she was eating enough? Did she think he would be angry with her because she wasn't? I thought her reaction foolish. Michael had been nothing but kind to her. Surely, he understood her thinness was a result of the cancer.

"Remember, don't put them in my trash can. Take it all home with you. Put them in your trash or keep them if you want."

I finished bagging the groceries and heated up some tomato soup. She filled the long pauses between each spoonful by nibbling on a cracker. "Remember how Mom always fixed tomato soup and crackers when we were sick?" I asked.

She forced a weak smile. She lifted the spoon as if the utensil were a five pound barbell. I couldn't pull my attention from her bone-thin arms.

When Michael and the rest of the family arrived, Margaret squared her frail shoulders and hung tough as usual. She spent the day outside on the patio as she observed her grandchildren splash in the kiddie pool and patter over a small wooden bridge spanning a bed of rocks designed as a creek. Occasionally chiming in on conversations, she grinned as the toddlers scrambled down the gravel paths, threading throughout the award-winning landscaped yard. After a lunch of hamburgers and hot dogs on the grill, I retreated to the den to check my email and message my Facebook friends.

Michael began cleaning up the kitchen, and I joined in. I rubbed his back as he bent over the sink, "It's been a nice day," I said as I finished up and gathered my things to head home, I asked, "How are you doing?"

Drying his hands, he threw down the towel and faced me, his features taut. "You and Gus need to make her eat," his red brows nearly met and the veins at his temples bulged. "She's not eating enough."

Surprised, I distance myself from the fire in his glare. Muscles in his jaw twitched. I reached across the distance I had created and placed my hand on his shoulder. "I know Michael, but that's part of the process. When Nate was dying…."

He jerked away from my touch. His eyes fired at me. "That was a long time ago! Things are different now! You have to make her eat!"

I glanced toward the patio door, surprised no one responded to his outrage. "Michael, she's not an animal. We can't force feed her."

He gripped the countertop, trying to control himself. The muscles in his neck flexed. "After her colonoscopy surgery, she would have died if I hadn't been taking care of her. You and Gus are letting her do whatever she wants!" His ruddy skin tone flashed redder.

A boulder dropped into the pit of my stomach. Acid burned my throat. I took a breath and swallowed. He's just a boy losing his mom.

"I know this is hard for you to watch, Michael. I understand. But you've got to allow her the dignity to die her way. If she doesn't want to eat, it's okay."

He slammed his fist on the counter. "No, it's not okay!"

Still, no response from outside.

He didn't cry. If he felt any heartache or fear, his rage stomped it down. His biceps bulged as he wiped down the kitchen counter.

Concern sprang up like an alarm going off. If I went home now, would Michael whisk her off to L.A? I crammed down my own hurt from his disapprova.l and steeled against his anger.

I refused to cry. I touched his rock-hard fist, poised on the counter. "Look, Michael, you're upset. Just promise me you'll ask her what she wants. Will you do that?"

His anger, cocked and loaded, caused his veins to pulse at his temples. He locked his knees and stood in a wide-legged stance. He didn't answer.

The memory of Mom standing over my eight-year-old self flashed into my mind when she had asked me who I wanted to live with if she divorced Dad. Michael's disapproval, like my mother's years ago, hit me hard.

I snapped back to reality. I stood before him, startled. I grasped hold of the counter and stared at Michael.

His angry attack magnified the dreaded lonely days which lay ahead. Margaret wasn't even gone, but already I was alone. I ached for someone to hold me, to tell me everything was going to be all right. That was not going to happen. That had been my sister's job. How am I ever going to survive without her?

I grabbed my keys and jacket and rushed out of the house.

Wiping away blinding tears, I sped home and pulled into the garage. The door rattled closed, shutting me off from the physical world, like my closet sanctuary when I was eight. No one could reach me. Solitude surrounded me.

Where was Marmalade? Usually I would call Margaret. But I couldn't do that anymore. I had to bear my own burdens. She didn't need to know how badly her son had behaved. Margaret had bigger problems.

How was I ever going to get through this? I collapsed on the couch, burying my face in my arms. Months of contained tears broke the floodgates which I had so carefully guarded. I sobbed and sobbed and sobbed.

Marmalade appeared from his own hidey-hole. He leaped up and landed, like a puffy cloud of cotton, beside me. His paw stroked my wet face and I pulled him close, hugging him. We lay there, Marmalade and I — long after my gulps for air subsided and darkness pulled the curtain on the day. "Who's going to have my back now, Marmalade?"

I gave Marmalade one last kiss and set him aside. Sitting up, I fumbled for the lamp switch. "No worry. I've always been independent." I've run my own business since I was eleven. Mom taught me well, I don't need anyone, I was grateful for Nate's dominating personality which had pushed me to stand up for myself.

Michael's true colors stirred a ripple of worry through me. He had painted the future, of this death watch. His attitude left space for more for blame and resentments, which now I knew were sure to come. My sister's reluctance to upset her sons, or go against their wishes was now understandable. She was not like me, she did not have the fortitude to face the kind of aggression I had just witnessed. What if Margaret died on my watch? A shiver raked over me. Would Michael shift the blame to me and not the cancer?

I dismissed the foreboding. I'd deal with Michael. He was young. He believed he had all the answers. I've dealt with criticism and judgement since I was sixteen. I wasn't going to let it get me down now. I wasn't what people said about me. He was losing his mother. I'd suck up my own hurts and resentments, for Margaret's sake.

But any sentimental scenario I had clung to, that my sister's transition would go smoothly, I now knew had been a foolish fairy tale.

CHAPTER NINETEEN
2015

I knew she would be late for our lunch date. Ashley was a last minute kind of person, usually fifteen or twenty minutes late. From past experience, I grew tired of sipping coffee alone in the restaurant until she arrived. I waited in the car. Today she showed up shortly after I did. Still, I waited. Her head bobbed around inside the car for another five minutes while she rummaged around in the clutter, searching for something. I described her as scattered, like her things.

Over the years, we had traveled many miles together each in our own motorhomes, from coast to coast and north to south. We had hashed over every subject under America's skies. We became accepting of each other's habits, likes and dislikes. I teased her about her habit of waiting to put things away until later, and she in turn, taunted me about my dogged determination to have "a place for everything and everything in its place." One day riding in her Prius, sightseeing, I held up my empty water bottle. "Where would you want me to put this? Do you have a trash bag?" I asked.

"Just toss it in the back," she said.

I shot her a troubled look as she maneuvered onto the freeway. "No really. Where?" I said.

She glanced at me and grinned. "Yes, really. Just toss it."

"I can't do that," I said. The thought of throwing trash into a pile of already disarrayed possessions scattered willy-nilly in the back seat grated against my code, "a place for everything and everything in its place." And she knew it. She couldn't hold back a devilish grin.

"Don't you have a bag for trash?"

She snatched the bottle from my hand. With a flick of her wrist, she flipped it, sending it, over the seat and into depths of clutter. Her little dog ducked as the plastic missile sailed over the spare tire and past the potted lettuce plants she grew for her canary and cockatiel. Missing a basket of dirty laundry, the bottle landed next to a pair of muddy hiking shoes and a bag of dog food.

Today, when she finally climbed out of her Prius, she stuffed a jacket back inside as I opened my car door. Turning to me, she chuckled. "Sorry to keep you waiting. I couldn't find my wallet."

When we finished ordering, I delved into the details of my day with Margaret's family and the blow-by-blow report of Michael's tirade.

"You didn't argue with him? That's good," Ashley said. "I'm not so sure I could have kept my mouth shut if my nephew talked to me like that."

"It wasn't easy, but I knew he was upset and hurting about his mom. He's so young. …."

"He's twenty-five."

"I know, but she's sheltered them. I don't think any of them know how to deal with any kind of feelings, certainly not anything of this magnitude."

"Death brings out the worst in people. I've seen some pretty ugly behavior when I volunteered for hospice."

"I'm not saying it didn't hurt …what he said. I went home and cried my eyes out. I'm surprised how I reacted."

"You're losing your sister. No one's considering your feelings — what you're going through. They're insensitive." Ashley scooped up refried beans onto her tortilla chip.

I shot Ashley a grim smile. "I forget that minor detail." Hearing Ashley point out my part in this family dance hit home. "I'm so busy handling everything, I forget why all this is happening."

"Staying busy is a way to cope." Ashley said.

I sighed and slumped back in the booth.

I laughed. "Well then, Margaret is helping me cope.Every morning Margaret has this inane list of chores for me to perform. She worries she's going to run out of pain medication so she requests every day that I count how many pills she has left. Because of the drugs she's on, she can't remember the tally and then insists I count them again. She insists on an inventory of her colostomy bags, too. She makes meticulous notes in her appointment book, but in her drugged state, she doesn't trust her notes so she asks me to count them again."

I had my own long inventory of complaints. How many times had I reiterated each one to Ashely?

"Margaret doesn't trust me to manage the drugs. She always asks Michael to check. She puts me on the same level with the uneducated hospice workers who bathe her and prepare her meals."

"Anyway, Michael certainly brought my feelings to the surface. I haven't cried like that since she was diagnosed."

"That's good. You need to cry."

"I drove back by her house later that night because I was afraid Michael might still be there, packing up her things and hauling her back to L.A. with him."

I grabbed the last chip and loaded it with salsa. "When I went home I called her. I told her I thought the day went well and asked if she needed anything, feeling her out. Everything was fine she said. So I assume she didn't hear him shouting at me."

Ashley smirked. "Or she didn't want to admit she heard him."

I laughed. "Maybe so, but I'll let it go. This is not about me, right? That's what you told me. It's about Maggie. That's the only reason I'm tolerating his disrespect."

"I'm thinking about asking Michael to come stay the weekends in order to give me a break. This is getting to be too much for me. Anyway, I think as her son ,he should be doing more."

Ashley tittered. "That ought to be interesting. I want to know how that goes down."

"I'll let you know. I feel like if I do, I'll be rocking the proverbial boat,but it is just getting too much for me. I need a couple days off."

"The Shanty Shaker RV group is having a campout next week at the flower fields in Carlsbad. I'm going. Maybe you should, too. It's not that far."

"I'd love to, but for now, I don't think so." I leaned back in the booth and sighed. "I'll pass. But I'll tell you one thing, when this is all over, you won't be seeing me around here. I'm hitting the road. There will be nothing to hold me back."

"Do you have your first trip planned?"

"I told Margaret that I was going to go back to Springfield. I promised to visit our old haunts and think of her, where we went sledding, ice skating and crawdad fishing. I'm looking forward to that."

"Like a memorial trip," Ashley said.

"Yes. I've always wanted to do Rte. 66. After that? Who knows?"

"I might join you," Ashley said. "I've always wanted to travel the Mother Road."

"That would be nice. I don't know why, but this being alone shit is really beginning to bug me. "

"You've been alone."

"I know. But it's different, now. I'll *really* be alone.... without my sister to talk to.

"You'll be fine."

"I know. I strongly believe if I just get through all this, something wonderful and good is going to come out of it. I feel it in my core. I've learned to thank God for the good and the *seemingly* bad. I've discovered the bad has always — ALWAYS — turned out to be the best thing that has ever happened to me. I don't know what the *good* is going to be, probably that I will be free to travel and write. That will be great. I couldn't ask for more."

"Did you talk to Margaret about finding your daughter?"

"Yes, but Margaret feels the same as I do. We figure if Charlotte were clean and sober she would have contacted one of us. Margaret doesn't want any more drama in her life and I agree."

"So you're not going to look for her?"

"I will. After Margaret passes. I'm not angry anymore. I want to .... I need to .... make my amends to her. But for now, this is all I can handle.

CHAPTER TWENTY
1964

No one spoke of the pregnancy. I bought a little white dress, but not a wedding dress. Mom planned the venue, the food and the announcements. Dad arranged for us to move into the basement apartment on Fourth Street. I didn't see Randy until we walked down the aisle. We didn't kiss after our vows.

For seven months, we played house although he never touched me. Randy went out drinking every night with his friends and returned stumbling down drunk by dawn. Sometimes he didn't show up for days. I held no delusions about the marriage. I didn't care.

I returned to school after Christmas break but morning sickness and extreme drowsiness overcame me like a powerful drug. It became more and more difficult to wake up early enough to be on time for my first class and then I couldn't keep from dozing off in class. I finally dropped out.

Without school to fill my time I groomed dogs to pay the rent. I cleaned my little apartment, burnt meals and turned up the volume on my radio at night to drown out the sounds of the ghostly clanking pipes and creaking walls that haunted the basement of the old Victorian house.

Randy had long ago stopped coming around. I often wondered if my father had threatened him.

The blustery winter gave way to tornados in the spring and a humid Illinois summer. Time dragged. Family picnics became my only outings. Conversations were limited to, "When are you due?" or "Do you want a boy or a girl?" If anyone wanted to know how married life was treating me, or if I was sorry I dropped out of school, or what was I going to do with my life, they never asked. No one inquired, "Are you happy?" Or "Where's your husband?" Or "I imagine this has been hard for you, how are you doing?" Like the marriage, I harbored no expectations that anyone might care about what I was going through. Mom and Dad, even Margaret, never asked. Why should anyone else?

I wanted a girl. I liked the name Charlotte. I knew nothing about raising a boy, but then I knew nothing about babies either. I had never dressed up dolls or babysat, and I never played house.

I wanted to go back to school.

I wanted to go horseback riding with the wind in my face.

I wanted to go sledding and pick ice balls off my mittens.

I wanted to float in an inner tube down the Sangamon River with Dad or lay in a bed of clover and dream of being in love.

I wanted to hang out with my friends, Barbara and Tamara.

I wanted to see Gary.

But I was tainted goods now. I was off limits. Everything was out of my reach.

When my water broke, it was time to pay the price of my decision. I was seventeen and scared. Mom drove me to the hospital and stayed with me. Dad was gone on his annual prospecting trip to Arizona. The ten hours in delivery rushed by for a seventeen-year-old who had no idea what to expect. A letter came from Dad. He congratulated me and said, "Make sure you are careful next time."

Cradling my baby in her arms, the nurse leaned down. The woman's crisp white uniform swished as she placed the bundle in my arms. "You have a beautiful baby girl," she said.

I wished I had played with dolls.

The red-faced package with puckered ruby lips reached her miniature hand out in my direction as if she knew me. Waves of motherhood washed over me. I fingered each delicate, pink body part, her ears and her baby hands and toes. A thousand dreams for her future burst into my heart. I promised myself that I would face all the responsibilities lying before me. For the first time in my life, someone needed me. I named her Charlotte.

Randy hadn't been home in months. With pressure from Mom and Dad, I agreed to divorce him. They handled the paperwork, filing the forms through their lawyer. I signed what they put before me. I hadn't needed Randy then, and I didn't need him now.

Charlotte slept in a bassinet next to my bed. At night, every four hours, I lifted her out and lay her beside me to nurse. When she wasn't nursing, she slept, dirtied her diapers and cried.

I spent much of my time at Mom and Dad's while Mom cooed and purred over her grandbaby, offering me advice about colic, which drove me into a frenzy, about what to feed her, and how to burp her. When Dad returned home from Arizona, I caught him gazing into her big round eyes while she gurgled and kicked in response to his babbling words.

I planned to return to school after winter break but discovered the educational system did not welcome diversity. Only one black student, a female, attended my high school, the rest attended the East side, where the lower income families like Randy attended. Because the girl was the daughter of a prominent local physician, her credits overruled the status quo.

The list of exceptions to the school's strict rules for returning was short. Pregnancy out of wedlock, marriage and divorce, or single motherhood were definitely not exceptions to the rules. But Dad visited the principal and made a deal.

They agreed to allow me to return, but with restrictions. They did their best to make me invisible to the school population as if I had the plague. My attendance at social functions — dances, games and clubs were forbidden. During assemblies and rallies the principal assigned me to wait in the office. I accepted the terms like the Emperor wearing his new clothes. Everyone agreed they saw the scarlet letter that I didn't wear.

I imagined the high school staff relished in their wisdom of solving their complicated problem. I did my time in the principal's office, studying at a corner table, as the staff marched past, entering and exiting my holding cell.

On my first day back, I stopped in the women's bathroom between classes. Stepping up to the basin alongside one of the most popular girls, Kathy Oakland, I washed my hands. Kathy's popularity came from cheerleading and a position on the student council. She brushed her rich auburn hair, which flowed down the middle of her back to her waist. She stuffed her brush into her purse and smoothed wrinkles from her fashionable pleated skirt. Her friends usually surrounded her, but not this day. She eyed me in the mirror. "Hi Janice."

I met the reflection of her gaze in the mirror, then she shifted her attention from the mirror to me and our eyes met.

"Welcome back," she said and smiled.

I held her gaze. I tried to return the smile. My throat clamped shut. She expressed a pleasant sincerity in those two words that had been absent since this nightmare had begun ten months ago. I was not invisible to her.

I flushed as I fought back tears. Gripping my purse, I managed to squeeze out a thank you.

Dragging my sweaty palms across my skirt, I wheeled around and shoved open the bathroom door. Choking down strong emotions, I rushed down the hall to my next class.

CHAPTER TWENTY-ONE
2015

I swiped at the years of guilty tears now soaking my face and dialed Ashley. Charlotte was barely sixteen the day I gave up on her. Today felt like that day. The three-decade old memory was as clear as if it were happening today.

Ashley's perky voice "Hi. What's up?"

"Are you busy?"

"Not at all. Just got back from a walk with Tika. She ate some kind of bone while I was talking to a couple camped a few spaces down." Ashley giggled.

"I'm amazed she has lived so long," I said. She eats everything. I would think you would have had a serious vet bill since you've owned her. "

"I know. It's a miracle. How's your sis doing?"

"She getting weaker and weaker. I'm afraid to leave her alone. I talked to her this morning and asked her if I could call Michael and ask him to start coming weekends in order to give me some relief."

I didn't mention to Ashley that Margaret wasn't very awake when I put the question to her.

"What did she say?"

"She said, 'I guess so. But I don't think he can.'"

I didn't tell Ashley that I didn't wait around for any discussion. I dashed out of the bedroom. I felt like a piece of shit. A stinking quitter.

"He should be helping. It's his mother. You're too old to carry the entire load."

"I have a bad feeling. I'm rocking the boat." My stomach cramped just thinking about calling Michael. Worst case? He would move her to his house. Margaret had always been clear, but only to me, that was not what she wanted. But if he insisted I was sure she wouldn't resist. "So what did he say?"

"I haven't called him yet."

I hunched over the kitchen table, wrestling with worry. Stretching to loosen the tired ache in my shoulders, I yawned and gulped down the last shot of caffeine in coffee cup. I couldn't shake the lurking mood of failure and disappointment.

From the beginning, I promised myself I would take care of her during her final days and keep her comfortable. Caring for my Nate had been emotional as well, but I had been there for him through his final days. I berated myself.

Damn it! I snatched up the phone from the table. Gripping it, I sucked in a deep breath. I couldn't put it off anymore. Anyway, the responsibility of my sister's care should not be all on my shoulders. I punched out Michael's number.

"Hi Janice. Is everything all right with my mom?" His question surprised me. Michael never asked about her. But then I had never called him, either.

Until now. Breaking the unspoken rules was not in this family's game plan.

But Margaret's weakness had progressed. The odor of stale heated air, the quiet of drugged sleep and the sensation of my sister's desperation, met me every day when I visited.

"She's doing as well as can be expected, I said. I waited for him to respond. Nothing. I took a deep breath and dove in. "The problem is me. Her care is getting too much for me. I really could use a break. I wondered if maybe you could start spending the weekends with her?"

I clutched the phone. There, I'd said it. I rocked the boat. I braced for his response.

"Sure," he said. "Tonya and I were just talking about doing that. We figured Mom's spare bedroom could be the baby's nursery."

I flopped back against my chair and exhaled the breath I'd been holding. "Thank goodness," I said. "That will be such a help. And maybe we could hire someone for two other days?" I knew money wasn't a problem. "Thank you, Michael. I'm sorry to have to ask but it is just getting too much for me."

"That's fine. I'm coming to see Mom tomorrow. I'll talk to her."

When I ended the call, I slumped over the table and rested my forehead on my crossed arms. Relief replaced the tension in my shoulders.

Any doubts about Michael's maturity faded. His supportive attitude eased my guilt. I had judged him too harshly. Maggie had raised her boys well. When needed, they were going to step up to the plate. Who would have thought it would play out so well? Not me.

CHAPTER TWENTY-TWO
1964

Rushing from the girls' bathroom, I fought emotional tears.Until now I had been able to I steel up against what people thought of me. But kind words? I didn't know how to deal.I shoved my way through the crowded hall. Rounding the corner, I collided with a student. "Sorry," I said without looking up.

On impact, my body reacted to the familiar scent before my brain recognized it was Gary. I swallowed hard. My face burned hot and I peered up. "Sorry," I said, again. Moving to the side, I stepped to move around him, but he blocked my path.

"I want to talk to you," he said.

The slight upturn of his mouth, again, made me weak and speechless

"Oh." I looked around. Nine months of shame and embarrassment rushed through me. I wanted to run. What could he possibly want from me? No one wanted me around them anymore. Students pushed past.

"Can I come by and see you?"

It had been almost a year. He stood taller than before. More confident. So much had happened. Did he know? Surely, he knew. Everybody knew. My pulse raced. Was it excitement? But my face burned with shame. I hung my head. My heart took over. I nodded and whispered, "Sure."

He pulled my chin up, forcing me to look at him, like he used to when he was going to kiss me. Was he going to kiss me right there in the hall? Of course not. I was tainted goods. Didn't he know that?

"I'll come over tonight."

"Okay." I tried to push past him. This time he let me. He started down the hall. I swung around. "Wait! You don't know where I live."

He turned to me, walking backwards. His smile told me he did. "I know."

I nodded.

"See you later."

I stared at his tight-ass jeans as he pushed through the swinging hall doors and out into the alley.

I only had morning classes. At noon I rushed to my car, sped across town to my parents, while my swelling breasts, begging for relief, leaked, Charlotte's crying confronted me as I burst through the back door. Tossing my books on the kitchen table, I ripped open my blouse while Mom bounced Charlotte in her arms, trying to appease her granddaughter's hungry demands. The crying raked across my new motherly nerves.

When Charlotte's ruby lips latched on to my nipple and began her furtive suckling, only then did I lean back and relax.

Mom hustled around in the kitchen. "I gave her oatmeal earlier, hoping it would satisfy her till you got here. I'll make you a sandwich."

"Thanks Mom." I hoisted Charlotte to my shoulder and patted her back. "She usually falls asleep by the time I get back to the apartment. I've got to get home. I've got a lot of homework." I didn't mention I hoped to get it done before Gary came over.

It was late, almost ten. I had given up on him and changed to pajamas. The Chevy's headlight lit up the street curb, only for a moment, then darkness overtook. A couple of soft barrum-barrums from the Chevy filtered across the yard and down the steps of my basement apartment, rattling the door. Then silence.

I didn't wait for his knock, I opened the door. Quiet electricity carried by the bitter arctic air from outside charged into my tiny apartment. The scent of leather followed him as he stepped over the threshold. My skin prickled. The grind of his coat's zipper, the creaking of his motorcycle jacket, and my heavy pulse, which pounded in my ears all amplified the silence. Slipping out of the icy garment, he handed it to me. I hugged it to my chest, its lining hot to touch. He looked around. "This is nice."

"Thanks."

I stood like an oaf, my feet frozen in place.

He stepped closer, taking his coat from my clutches and draped it across a dinette chair.

"May I see your baby?"

I came to. "Charlotte?"

"Yes." He stepped closer, grinning at my nervousness. "Is that what you named her? I like it."

I rubbed my sweaty hands against my pj's pink flannel with kittens frolicking and dancing on its fabric.

I scurried to the bedroom. "She's sleeping." I switched on a small lamp on the antique vanity. The soft yellow glow spread across my bed and into the bassinet. I came around beside Gary as he leaned in for a closer look. "Would you like to hold her?"

He straightened. "Oh, I don't know."

"It's okay. You won't wake her. Her belly's full and she sleeps through the night now." I reached in and gathered her up. "Here."

He opened his arms and I placed the precious bundle in them. "Just support her head, like this." I placed his hand under her head and neck.

He touched her button nose and fingered her tiny ears. The lamplight illuminated his look of amazement. "She's so small,"

"She's grown. You should have seen her when she was born."

"She's beautiful." He whispered and handed her back. I placed her in the bassinette and turned to him. We stood so close our bodies touched. I held my breath.

He kissed me. Lightly at first, not demanding, as if unsure. My heart exploded while my legs turned to jello. He still liked me. I was not tainted goods to him. I kissed him back. A flashfire welled up inside me healing the hurt and bringing a sense of belonging. The world around me softened. A deep contentment overcame me, satisfying a need for which I had been unaware I had longed.

He kissed me again and then again, each time harder than the last. I returned them with equal passion. We collapsed onto the bed.

No curfew, no flashing porch light was going to stop us this time. His hands slid under my pajama top, exploring, circling, and finding my swollen breasts. I pressed up against his chest, wanting to return the soaring sensations he stirred in me. My hand probed under his sweatshirt. A ringing in my ears made me deaf to everything but his moans.

He entered me like Randy, but this time my body knew the reward. I met his thrusts. We rose and fell, enjoying the sweet agony of our heated race to the finish line.

Just when I felt the finish line so close that I thought I might explode from one more thrust, he stopped.

"I've got to quit," he said and pulled away.

I sat up like a spring that had been sprung. "Did I do something wrong?"

His brow furrowed. Shaking his head, he gathered me into his arms. "Oh no, babe. You did everything right." His features softened and smiled as he titled my chin up and kissed me. "I had to pull out. You don't need to get pregnant again."

"Oh!" I swallowed hard and hung my head. How could I have not thought of the consequences?

He climbed out of bed, stepped into his jeans, and stuffed his hardness inside. My pulse throbbed, again. "I should go," he said as he pulled his sweatshirt down over his head.

Coming around to my side of the bed, he pushed back the tousled hair from my face and hugged me. "You're amazing," he said and kissed me. "I should go."

The door closed quietly behind him.

CHAPTER TWENTY-THREE
2015

The next day, feeling renewed that Michael was going to step up to the plate, I took advantage of his visit and ran the errands I had been putting off. I walked with a lightness I hadn't felt for some time, knowing I was no longer alone on this death watch. I loaded the last of the groceries into the trunk. Slamming the lid, I reached for my cell in response to Margaret's ringtone which sang out Rascal Flatt's, *Here Comes Goodbye*. What can I say? I have a morbid sense of humor.

"How was your visit with Michael?" I smiled, proud for her that she had such a responsible son.

"I'm going to go live with him."

What?

Like a sucker punch, her words knocked me off balance. I staggered. I must have misunderstood. "What?" This time I it said out loud.

My mind spun out of control, trying to make sense of the sudden turn of events. My brain swept over the last months, grasping for answers. What happened to Michael's declaration of helping out on the weekends?

"Don't consider it a punishment," she said.

Whaa....? Why? .... Why would I think that? Did *she* think that? Who was punishing who? Maggie didn't want to go to her son's home. She had hated it during her six-week struggle, recovering from her colostomy operation. She had been very clear to me about her wishes. "I want to die at home," she had said.

The shocking turn of events tangled up in my brain. I felt dizzy. "What?" I said again, as I choked back everything I was thinking and clutched the phone so hard my fingers hurt. "Why?"

"What was I supposed to do?" Her weak voice was soft, but she spat out the question with a surprising bitterness. "When you come to me out of the blue and tell me you're done? That you just can't do this anymore!? What was I supposed to do?"

Margaret pressed on. "You could have discussed it with me. All you have ever told me was how happy you are to be able to be here for me. Then you hit me with, 'I quit?' I can't take this anymore?' I had no clue. What was I supposed to do?"

My fingers ached. I fumbled with the car door and yanked it open. Sinking into the driver's seat, I stared out into the parking lot. She was angry, but hurt and fear is what I heard in her voice. I had handled this terribly wrong.

I expected a negative reaction from Michael, but not from Margaret. I knew she was adamant about not bothering Michael, afraid to burden him. When I had asked Margaret if I could ask Michael to come weekends, I distinctly recalled her answer. "You can ask him," she said. "But I don't think he can," she had said.

What had happened during Michael's visit? I hadn't forgotten how his behavior had switched to psycho mode months ago. I spoke slowly. "I did not say,' I quit', or 'I can't do this anymore. ' I said. 'It's getting too much for me. I need help.' I asked you if it was all right to see if Michael could spend the weekends with you. I remember your answer. You said, 'Yes. You can ask him, but I don't think he can.'"

"You threw it at me. What was I supposed to say? You said, 'I can't take this anymore. I quit'."

Now my own anger began to simmer. "I did not say 'I quit.' You might have taken it that way, but that is not what I said and certainly not what I meant. I'm sorry you misunderstood and that I didn't make it clear."

"You said you had enough. You can't take it anymore."

My fingers ached, reminding me to loosen my grip on my cell. "I'm telling you right now. I never intended to walk away." Now my words were tight and clipped. "I just need help. I'm sorry I if didn't make it clear."

"You said you had enough. You said, 'I quit.' That's what you said."

"I am telling you, one last time, I did not say those words. You interpreted it that way. If you insist I did, then you're calling me a liar. And if you say it again, I'm going to hang up."

"What was I supposed to do? Why didn't you tell me it was getting too much for you?" Her frail voice squeaked.

"I did. Many times. I asked you to have Michael get the cell phone battery for you. I asked you to have him water the plants and go to the store for you when he visited. Your answer was always, "I don't want to bother him." I also asked if we could hire someone. You nixed that too."

A long silence passed. When she spoke, I strained to hear her softened voice. "That's true." Her voice cracked. I thought of a precious heirloom crashing to the floor and scattering in pieces. She whispered as if there was no air to breathe. "I didn't know what else to do," she said. "He told me to either go into a home or come live with me."

I cringed. "Can I come over? Give you a hug?" Like a cornered animal her hurt and fear clawed at my heart. My time with her now had an end date.

"I would like that," she said.

I pulled into her driveway and parked. *You've gone and done it now, Janice. You won't be making this one-mile trek much longer.*

Inside, I crept into the darkened bedroom, like a whipped dog. She watched me approach, her sunken eyes boring into me. I leaned down and hugged her. We held the embrace, neither of us wanting to let go. She had trusted me. I had blown it. Now, even more so, I wanted every possible minute with her. "I know this isn't what you wanted, Maggie," I said. "But it will be a good. Michael needs this time with you, whether he knows it or not. It will be good for the both of you." She raised her hairless brow in doubt. "Michael said he will move everything in this room so it will all be the same at his house."

Sure, that will fix everything.

We both grew quiet. We knew it wouldn't be the same. Nothing would ever be the same again.

Frightened and defeated, Margaret was facing the last leg of her journey — back to L.A.

She squeezed my hand. "We can talk on the phone anytime. You can go on your trip, now. It'll be okay."

She was comforting me?

"If I forget anything here at the house, Gus can bring it when he visits." She pulled me down close and kissed me.

"And, like you said, the hospice will be better in L.A.," I said. "You won't have to worry anymore." A guilty spark of relief stirred inside me. The responsibility of her care was no longer mine.

The thought of LA hospice caregivers must have comforted Margaret. She closed her eyes and nodded.

I couldn't wait to get away from this unpredictable family, from Michael. A wave of guilt made me faint.

I stayed with Margaret until her boyfriend, Gus, arrived. She hadn't yet broke the news to him that she was moving back to L.A. I felt worse for him than I did for me. He, too, was losing her before she was gone. He had lost three wives. I sensed Margaret was going to be his hardest loss. I knew he would make the grueling drive to L.A. to visit, which only made me feel worse. He was eighty-six.

After Gus arrived I returned home and sat alone in the dark house. The weight from the responsibility for Maggie's care had been lifted. Did I feel better? No.

I felt like shit. It was happening again. Thirty-five years ago, I had been unable to handle the responsibility of my own daughter. I had given up on Charlotte.

Now, I had given up on Maggie. Her family had me in a vise. Was I supposed to make that taxing drive back and forth to L.A. to visit her? I couldn't. I should. What would people think if I didn't? I already knew.

I sat outside on the chaise lounge, my knees to my chest, watching the daylight brighten as I sipped my morning coffee. I hadn't slept. I rubbed my dry, scratchy eyes. Could she even handle the move to L.A.? She was so weak.

I had been foolish, asking for help. What was wrong with me? I cared for Nate until the end. Why couldn't

I now? That was ten years ago, for goodness sake! You're going to be seventy.

Not too old to go traipsing across the country in your motorhome. Gus is 86.

It didn't matter. The game had been called. The criticism, the doubt, the lack of emotional support, as well as the wrenching ache of watching Maggie fade away, left me empty. I had nothing left.

My cell dinged, pulling me away from my dilemma. I had mail. I clicked on the app. It was Michael. Good. He must be calling to explain his bizarre change of plans.

"I wanted to update you," the text began. *"I had a nice visit with mom yesterday. I told her she could either move into a home or move in with me. She is going to move in with me but I won't be able to move her for two weeks. I hope you can hang in there that long and not drop her like a hot potato on my doorstep."*

WHAT!! The passive-aggressive shit! Fuck him!

Voices from my pushed me down.

You're stupid… you're a fraidy cat. You always were a Daddy's girl…!!

I rose up. Fuck Michael!

Maggie is his mother! He and Daniel should be taking care of her.

CHAPTER TWENTY-FOUR
1964

Dad had been right. Life was no longer simple. I carried a full load at school and kept the same pressure on in summer school. I dropped Charlotte off at my folks while I took the necessary high school college prep classes. My afternoons left little room for anything but caring for the Charlotte and cramming in homework when she napped. I graduated with a 3.0 grade point average and was accepted at the University of Illinois for the fall semester.

Gary came by the apartment some evenings. He chipped in, rocking Charlotte when she fussed and even attempted a few feeding sessions. When

Charlotte was down for the night we switched gears. Experimenting in the bedroom kept us wanting more and more from one another.

I graduated with no pomp or circumstance, picking up my diploma from the principal's office where I had done my penance. The principal's secretary was a washed-out blonde with thin-lined lips and facial features suggesting she had trudged through her fifty years of life on a slow revolving treadmill. When she caught sight of me her lip pursed even tighter.

A frown pinched her forehead into deep wrinkles. She fiddled with a pile of paperwork, tapping the stack sharply against her desk. Her muddied-grey chopped curls dangled over her forehead. A couple strands caught in the deep crevises. The polka-a-dots of her polyester dress were oblong, stretched taut around her thick trunk. The pinch-lipped woman's aloofness struck me, like a sucker punch, as it had every time I entered the office.

At first, I thought she didn't see me standing at the counter. But then she rose, and reaching behind her, pulled at the back of her dress, which had embedded in her tight ass. She clip-clopped across the office and approached the counter that walled her off from life's reality and me.

Separated by the two feet of the counter, she stood before me — the front-runner for the high school staff. She still refused to look at me as if I were one of the mangy dogs I groomed. I wanted to rush at her, like I might attack her. I wanted to ask her if she had ever gotten laid.

"I'm here to pick up my diploma," I said.

"Oh." Her squeaky voice surprised me. We had never spoken. She reached under the counter, pulled out a folder and straightened to her full height.

She slapped the evidence of my greatest life achievement onto the Formica. The narrow line of her lips screwed downward even farther. That surprised me, too, as if it pained her to shove the diploma across the space to me.

"Here you go." She snapped out the words, the timbre of her voice like a bad note on a violin and just as annoying.

She slid the proof of my long struggle across the army-green counter as if it were only a detention slip. I stared at her because I could. She refused to look at me. Her attitude, her squinty dark eyes, her thick, stiff stature represented everything I had suffered through. — The sting of my classmates when they turned away as I passed them in the hall. — The burning shame which the school, my family and friends instilled on me with their silent judgements — all of it.

The woman not only acted not only as the principal's sentry, but also as the world's guardian. She was the gatekeeper. She decided who entered the garden of the pure and good and who did not. The bitch mirrored my father's attitude. Dad had wanted to send me away. He wanted me to give Charlotte up for adoption — an easy solution to his embarrassing situation. He wanted to cast me off, the same way he took out the garbage.

I picked up the leather bound document and cradled the diploma with both hands as if it were as important as the Senators cherished State Championship football trophy displayed behind glass in the awards case across from the office.

I ran my fingers over the gold letters embedded on the plush cover of the booklet. *Springfield High School*. Opening it, I studied my name written in calligraphy.

I had done it. I graduated.

All at once the realization struck me. Until right now, I had bought into society's lie. I believed I was the slut whom everyone saw when they looked at me. Until now, they had convinced me. I believed I would end up a high school dropout, living in a trailer on welfare with a hassle of kids and another one on the way.

I softly closed the book, which represented my monumental achievement. Pride shot through me. I looked up, ready to challenge the stout woman's puffy, pouty face, but she had already returned to her desk and was busying herself, shuffling through her pompous paperwork.

I straightened and spun around. Pushing back my shoulders, I raised my chin. Slamming the thick oak door with the frosted glass window, I marched past the gilded trophy case, down the hall, and strode out into the fresh air. I blinked in the sunlight. I had beat the odds. I was a high school graduate.

The University of Illinois at Champaign-Urbana campus had accepted me for the fall semester. A student with a baby would not be allowed to reside in the dorms but I no longer shared anything with girls my age. I didn't care. They wore out subjects about clothes and tittered tirelessly over the boys burning rubber from the stop signs by the women's track.

I had my own car and I knew what the boys wanted. They were not going to get it from the girls who were still performing their flirty-girly dance which Barbara and I had stepped to two years ago, a time in my life that now felt like an old movie.

Last year, during Margaret's sophomore year she had met a veterinary undergrad and married him. They lived in a seedy trailer park off campus and planned to move to northern California to attend Davis University to complete his graduate work in veterinary medicine.

Dad found a mobile home for me on the outskirts of town in a quiet tree-lined trailer park. The all-aluminum Spartan trailer nestled on a grassy space, among the shade trees. It's rich, warm Cherry wood interior and the u-shaped breakfast nook added a sit-for-awhile feeling. A full-sized bed in the rear bedroom left just enough room to squeeze around in order to make it. The single bed in the middle of the trailer would be perfect for Charlotte's room. Another single bed in the front bedroom had been removed, replaced by a small couch, turning the space into a cozy study.

My senior high school schedule had left me little time to consider what the small minds thought of me. I learned to steel against the looks and murmurings and not to care. I spent my time after school and on weekends, caring for Charlotte, doing homework, and while Mom babysat, grooming dogs. The money I earned was going to be more than enough for trailer park rent and gas.

The one-week break between summer school and when my college classes began, gave me just enough time to settle into my new college residence.

To pay for the trailer, I used the money from the sale of the house Margaret and I had purchased a lifetime ago. I told Dad I would earn my own money and make my own way. I planned to drive home on weekends to groom dogs. No one was going to tell me what to do or how to live my life.

Margaret had been right all along. Like her, I couldn't escape soon enough from Springfield with its small minded, up-tight attitudes. I couldn't wait to put a hundred miles distance from the cutting memories and the disappointment in Dad's eyes.

The last morning with Gary I wrote my new address on a piece of paper and handed it to him. "Write to me," I said. Rising on my tiptoes, I placed a quick kiss on his lips.

When I turned, he grabbed my arm, pulled me to him, and kissed me hard. My face heated and my pulse pounded as it always did when I knew he was aroused. He took my hand and pressed my hand against the hard bulge in his crotch. "Screw writing to you. I'll come see you."

CHAPTER TWENTY-FIVE
1964

Clutching my diploma and the taste of Gary still on my lips, I climbed into my compact blue American Rambler crammed tight with my apartment belongings. Charlotte gurgled baby sounds in her car seat next to me. Dad made his last check on the tires, oil and water. "You're good to go," he said, slamming the hood down and thumping it with his palm.

I was leaving Springfield with no intention of returning except on weekends to make the hundred-mile trek back to groom dogs. Margaret's nine-year-old declaration rang from the past when we sat cross legged in the neighbor's garden that night amongst the sweet scent of fresh tomatoes. Her words echoed in my head. "Someday I'm going to get out of this small-minded town."

I stepped on the gas and my little blue Rambler, loaded with what little I had accumulated during my short adult life, backed down the driveway away from my childhood home, with its two tiny bedrooms and the cherry tree and little the log cabin playhouse in the back yard.

Mom and Dad retreated into the house, but like my first date with Gary, I saw Dad's shadow as he watched from the living room window.

I was also leaving behind the teepees Margaret and I erected out of sun flower stalks in our neighbor's field.

The chance of ever dancing in flooded grassy ditches when it rained or of huddling in musty leaf caves in the fall or snow caves in the winter lessened with each increasing mile.

The drive through the old neighborhood, through town and over the country roads felt monumental. I wanted to remember every detail.

The farmland drifted past my windshield as I picked up speed on the highway and headed toward Champaign-Urbana. Charlotte slept with her thumb in her mouth and her finger hooked around her nose.

The wide-open spaces and the thousands of acres of corn and bean fields, stretched into infinity Cotton ball clouds dotted the blue horizon..

I had never considered the landscape before, but now I took note. The scent of sweet corn still hovered over the harvested, stubbled landscape.

The exposed, flat scenery fed my new sense of freedom. My pulse quickened as the miles clicked by. The distance increased between my past and me, I sat straighter. The feelings of guilt, shame and embarrassment faded the further I traveled. I glanced at the odometer. In sixty-eight miles, I would be on my own. I would be free.

I thought of my nights with Gary. I was going to miss him. Our evenings in that low ceilinged basement apartment, watching TV, making love and experimenting, had been a private world of our own. Just Gary, me and Charlotte.

I knew what people thought. Maybe Gary did too, but I had drawn strength from his presence. I wondered now, as the landscape drifted by, if I ever would have made it through that senior year without him.

For the first time someone enjoyed me and wanted my company. We didn't call it love. We never spoke of that. I learned a long time ago not to ask for anything more than what was given. But that precious time with him allowed me to drive society's damning voices from my head.

I eased my little car through the shady trailer park and found my new shiny aluminum Spartan mobile home. A myriad of motions swept over me as I balanced Charlotte on my hip and unlocked the door. Inside the deep cherry wood walls and gingham curtains surrounded me like a security blanket, no different than those childhood hours with my diary and books, huddled in the bedroom closet.

I set Charlotte on the braided rug and scattered a few toys in front of her while I began hauling clothes and the meager pieces of my life in from the car.

By late afternoon everything was in its place, I'd fed Charlotte and put her down for her nap in her new crib. When she woke I would dress and go into town to explore the campus and pick up a few groceries. I popped the cap off a Coke and scooted into the u-shaped dinette. As I scanned my new environment, I sighed with satisfaction. I was on my own.

The drive through the isolated campus, which would be hopping with activity on Monday when classes began, revealed only a trickle of students, strolling the sidewalks, which led from one classic building to another. I found the University daycare at the child development center where I would drop Charlotte in the morning while I attended classes.

The following morning went smoothly as I packed Charlotte's diaper bag loaded her in the car to drop her off at day care. As I hurried down the walkway to my first class, I passed twittering girls I guessed were freshmen like me, who obediently skipped down the path laid out for them as they giggled about their boyfriends and about this dance or that party.

It was 1964. The campus hummed with an electric sexual energy. Kennedy's assassination ended the Age of Innocence, and the Vietnam War escalated.

The emotions of war protestors and draft dodgers fueled rallies on campus and fed the free love fever. I was not in Springfield anymore.

But I rarely dated. The crass, collegiate-sweatered boys pranced and danced to the same tempo as their wide-eyed, golden haired girlfriends.

On weekends, Gary drove the hundred miles to see me as he said he would. If we went out, it was to a drive-in movie, because of Charlotte.

Tonight, Gary parked in the back three rows at the drive-in as usual as I reached over the front seat and cooed to calm Charlotte, fussing in her car seat in the back.

"Do you want anything from the snack bar?"

I didn't look up as I wiped off the pacifier and popped it into Charlotte's mouth. "Popcorn and a coke would be good."

"I'll be right back."

I turned to study his backside as he strode up to the concessions stand. My pulse spiked at the sight of him yet on the surface we had become comfortable, like a married couple.

When he returned, he balanced the Cokes as he handed me the popcorn through the drivers' window. I grabbed the popcorn and flipped the door handle, giving it a shove open.

Too hard!

Coke and crushed ice flew into the air. He gasped as the ice sloshed down the front of his bright white t-shirt. He threw the drinks to the ground.

"Oh dear! I'm sorry!"

"That's cold!" He yanked his shirt up and over his head. Wadding it up, he dabbed at the front of his jeans and then shot me a look of agitation. His blue eyes flashing in the darkness.

"Sorry!" I repeated. I reached over the front seat and snatched a diaper from Charlotte's bag and handed it to him. "Here! I said.

He took the diaper as he slipped into the driver's seat. I snatched the cloth from him. "Let me do that." I patted and rubbed until I felt the swell in his jeans.

"Maybe you should unbutton them," he said, his voice husky. He chugged a beer he'd opened before he had trekked to the concession stand and then tossed the bottle into a trash bag.

"Sure. Okay." I glanced up at him. "Do you think they'll dry faster?"

He smiled that special smile he used only for me. "Maybe," he grinned. "It's worth a try."

We played around hardly concentrating on the movie. While Charlotte slept in her car seat, we moved her to the front seat and climbed into the backseat, finishing what we had started.

Afterwards, propped on an elbow beside me, Gary smiled down "We should get married," he said.

We hadn't talked about love. "You're drunk," I laughed. He always joked around after a few beers. Anyway we were just having a good time. I kissed him deeply.

At some point during my freshman year, our interludes ended. Had the hundred-mile drive been too much? Had he lost interest? Had my rebuff of his marriage proposal hurt his feelings?

Whatever happened I never knew.

College life kept me busy. Classes and a part time job at the Physics Department filled my days. Caring for Charlotte and homework, took up my afternoons and evenings. Every Friday I drove the hundred miles back home. I groomed dogs all day on Saturdays and Sundays and then make the trek back toChampaign on Sunday night. There was little time for fun.

CHAPTER TWENTY-SIX

2015

Bursting to rehash the email from Michael, I couldn't wait to meet Ashley for lunch. We had been best friends for years, caravanning up and down and across the country in our motorhomes sharing our experiences and opinions. As members of a recovery program, we both practiced the no nonsense philosophy of the 12-steps. We rarely fed into each other's drama of the day.

I tapped my fingers as the waitress finished taking our order and tucked the tablet in her apron pocket.

"Will that be all?"

"We're good," I said, dismissing her. I waited for her to make her way to the next table and then shook the printed email in front of Ashley. "I can't believe he said that!. He was so pleasant the day before."

Ashley studied the letter. "Like a hot potato on his doorstep??" She teed heed and looked up at me. "That's classic passive-aggressive behavior." She slid the letter back across the table to me.

"Michael even told me he and Tonya had discussed making Margaret's extra bedroom into a nursery for Benny when the time came."

"I was so relieved. I had been afraid he'd get pissed and say she had to come live with him

"But why am I not surprised? According to Margaret, I was done, that I was walking away completely. Geez! I only asked for help on the weekends. These people are crazy! But i.m also relieved she's going to L.A. I've been worried for a long time that if Maggie died on my watch, they would blame me."

I slumped back in the booth. Tears burst like a floodgate had opened. "Punishment my ass." I said. "That's what Margaret said. "Why would she even think that?"

"So now what? Are you going to drive back and forth to LA to see her?"

"I can't imagine doing that every day. Every weekend is going to be bad enough. It's an hour and a half drive one way. And that's if there's no traffic, which never happens."

Ashley waited for me to finish my rant. "Didn't you stay once in their drive way in your motorhome?"

"Yes, but neither she nor Michael has suggested that. Anyway, I'm not sure I could deal with Michael even more day. He'd probably want me to take care of her 24/7 like he expected me to do here."

"Maybe you could find an RV park that's close."

"God! I don't want to do this. Margaret said it was okay if I go on my trip. We can talk on the phone anytime she said. She's saying I can go, that it's all right with her."

Are you going to go?"

"Why not? She'll be in L.A. She'll be happy, surrounded by all the people like her who are better than everyone else. I sure hope there's an L.A. Heaven when she dies, because she won't be happy anywhere else.

Margaret climbed into the passenger seat of her Lexus. Turning the ignition, I shifted the car into reverse and punched the garage remote several times but it didn't work. "Have you got the prescription from the doctor?" I asked.

Margaret fumbled through the paperwork she clutched. "Yes, it's here." She leaned back and sighed as I backed out of the garage. "I can't believe you're going to leave town so soon."

I punched the remote several more times before the door finally lowered. She should have bought a new garage door opener years ago, but she probably figured there will be a couple hundred bucks more for the boys to inherit. "You told me you'd be okay," I said, "that we can talk on the phone."

Watching the door creak close, Margaret stared through the windshield.

Or maybe she wished she'd replaced it so the boys wouldn't have to deal with it after she's gone. They are so busy.

"Anything that you might forget to take with you to LA, Gus can bring when he visits," I said.

A neighbor's leaf blower hummed from a yard down the street, accenting the silence in the car. My stomach knotted into a lead ball. "Like you said, we can talk on the phone anytime we want.". "Was there anything else you need me to do?" I prayed she didn't. "I guess not."

I didn't want it to end like this. Time was running out. Every second counted. Yet my desperate ache to hit the road and put as much distance between me and this tortured, sinking situation pulled at me. I wanted to scream.

A dank oppression hung heavily in the cushy space of the old Lexus. Was it my sorrow or Margaret's? Like a damp blanket, it hung in the air ready to enfold its cold corners around us. We rode to the dispensary avoiding conversation and commenting only on the weather and the traffic.

A cloud of dust swirled up when I turned off the asphalt road and into an unpaved parking lot. I eased past a rickety card table set up in the dirt with a couple guys in dread locks selling what looked like an assortment of car parts.

Dodging pot holes, I parked in front of a stucco shack. Its many cracks were patched with many shades of beige and an occasional pink or blue, and was probably the glue that kept the building standing. Plywood covered a front window and a blue tarp draped over a corner of the roof in hopes to protect from a rainfall that had not happened during the past four years of California's worst drought.

Margaret pressed her purse tight under her arm. "Make sure you lock the door. "She eased out of the car without taking her eyes off two bouncer-built men, flanking each side of the building's unpainted, warped door with bars on its one small window. Golden dust shadowed the black flared pants legs of the men's jeans.

On the left, a Shrek of a man, his mouth line small and tight like the Disney character, greeted my sister as she approached, "Good morning, ma'am," he said. Under a loose hanging, grey training jacket, the hulk's chest strained against a white compression shirt.

The other guard could have been his twin. He nodded. The door wobbled as the other brother pulled open the broken-down door. Although both men smiled graciously, they moved with a stiff readiness, communicating the strength and control of ex-military. Both meant business. Their presence alarmed me, but at the same time made me feel safe.

"The banks won't grant these places credit," my sister had explained last month during our first visit to purchase her medical marijuana. "They only take cash. Thus, the heavy security."

Not allowed to enter the product room without a prescription, I waited in the stark reception area as another employee led Margaret into the depths of the dispensary. I peered through a smeared glass window and watched. Two more men, much like the guards outside stood ready as she entered.

No investment had been made in the product room design. Rows of jars labeled and filled with buds of various strains of Cannabis lined the milky shelves of four scuffed and scarred glass display cases. I imagined this would be the furnishings' last gig before being retired to the dump.

Margaret finished her business. With the small white paper sacks tucked tightly under her arm, she pushed past the rickety door as I tracked behind her hurried footfall to the car. I sensed her urgency to get far away from this place with its worn out bones and disrepair which wailed with a sorrowful hopelessness.

Back in the car, Margaret held up one of the paper bags. "I want you to hide this bag up in the closet when we get home. Michael wanted me to get this for him."

"Pot?" I said, glancing at the bag.

"Yes," Margaret smiled at me. "He said, 'Make sure your sister doesn't smoke it all before I pick it up.'" She grinned at Michael's joke.

I gripped the steering wheel so tight my knuckles turned white while I waited for the traffic to clear. Unamused and too irritated to wait, I saw a narrow opening in the traffic and gunned the accelerator so hard gravel spewed out across the parking lot, spraying the dreadlocks tending to their auto parts business at the wobbly card table. "I haven't smoked the stuf in over fifty years," I said.

Margaret and all of her family considered me a fuck up. They always had. If I wasn't so angry I would have laughed at the irony. Just who is the fuck-up? Me? The owner of a prosperous business who is respected all across town? Am I the loser, who is debt free and with a padded savings account?

Or is Michael the loser with his credit so maxed out that he had to borrow money from his mommy? Is the loser the stay-at-home dad living off his wife's income in the big glittery town full of little white lies and all sorts of shiny things?

My fingers ached from gripping the steering wheel. "I haven't smoked the stuff in over fifty years," I said.

She should have bought a garage door opener with Michael's pot money.

Michael's marijuana usage explained a lot. Six months ago Michael had outlined his reasons to his mom for closing down his construction company – the economy, problems with employees, his bad back. He wrapped up his defense by hugging his son and delivering an emotional pitch about his desire to spend quality time with the toddler and now I know, to also smoke pot. He wanted to be a stay at home dad, he said. Tonya earned enough at Disney as a web designer. Michael didn't have to work. And anyway, he had an inheritance landing in his lap in the near future.

When Michael finished itemizing his problems and stress, Margaret gave him a warm embrace. He had made the sale. She only wanted her boy to be happy. But caring for Margaret? Michael could not know the task he was taking on. Michael would not be going out to play anytime soon. Watching his mother die and saying good bye would be hard, she had coddled him so.

I wondered if Michael thought his bedside manner and the LA doctors could save his mother? Perhaps Margaret would demand less of Michael. She respected his time more than mine. Or maybe now Margaret was resigned to play the cards she had been dealt. Maybe she had reached the acceptance stage of her journey.

CHAPTER TWENTY-SEVEN

No matter, I failed Margaret, and myself. Margaret wanted to die in her own home, and I wanted to care for her until the end. None of that was going to happen. And now, as I looked back, I might as well include Charlotte in my list of failures. No doubt, the family and everyone else felt the same. I was sixteen again, right back where I had started from — pregnant and beginning a career of disappointing everyone.

I'm sure my nephews resented me for sending Charlotte to live with them back then. And now they aren't happy again. I dumped my sister on them, too, never minding its their mother.

Margaret never had much fight in her to begin with. And now, she seemed defeated. Maybe that's why she agreed to return to Michael's. She was ready to surrender and it didn't matter whose roof she did it under.

The day came to say goodbye to Margaret and for her to move to L.A. I handed Margaret my house key in Michael's presence. If he believed I would steal his pot, he would also think me capable of stealing things from the house once Margaret was gone.

In the bedroom, Margaret and I clung to one another in a desperate hug which we knew might be our last.

I pulled away, unable to face her desperation. I felt somehow this was all my fault. If I had not asked for help, this move would not have happened.

I said goodbye, rushed out the front door.. I held back my tears back until I was in the car, rounding the corner and driving the long mile home.

I had been so full of myself, believing I was going to be such a positive influence during Margaret's transition, yet here I was, abandoning the death watch.

The day of freedom from caring for Margaret which I had been awaiting had come too soon. It wasn't supposed to end this way. My step was heavy as I stowed the last-minute items into the motorhome.

After making one more walk through the house, I climbed into the driver's seat and turned the ignition. The cold engine sputtered and labored. Did it feel the weight of extra baggage stowed away on this trip? I stomped the accelerator, as if to out run the unwelcome burden and sped away with a fervor that disgusted me.

As I crept through L.A'.s everyday congestion, I didn't fight the traffic, only my conscience. Vehicles tangled up at every major interchange in an effort to either take part in the city's hub bub, or to escape it.

White knuckling the steering wheel, I neared the exit to Michael's house with plenty of time to change lanes. I pictured Margaret sitting upright, pillows propped behind her, poised with that tilt of her chin and tight jaw as she struggled to regain her the thin shred of dignity which she'd spent on the move. But I remained in the second lane wrestling with myself, listening to the condemning voices droning in my ears and reliving the ugly visions of my past.

You could turn around.

The thought of calling off this mad stampede out of town sent a stab of pain through me because I knew it was an impossibility for me. Maybe for some one stronger, but not for me. I hunched over the wheel. I pictured entering Michael's house.

Would he look me in the eye? Would he feel at least a spit of guilt for the disrespect he had shown me? Could I contain my resentments? I don't think I ever would trust Michael, after his cutting remark about dropping Margaret on his doorstep like a hot potato.

I concentrated on the road ahead and tried to picture my destination — the wind-swept Westport Beach campground — the pounding surf and its rage and glory. I breathed in deeply, imagining the taste of the crisp, salty air. The cramping in my stomach loosened its hold.

I had wanted so much for things to be different.

You could go back. You should go back — for Margaret's sake.

The cramps returned.

Everyone I know would not do what I was doing. They would stay, ulcers or not and judge those who didn't remain. Like when I was sixteen, no one wanted to know what I was going through, they just wanted me out of sight. I gave them my rebellious finger then, and I guess that is what I am doing now. I'm walking away now — *at 60 miles per hour.*

On the other side of L.A. traffic opened up. By early afternoon, I arrived at the Elks lodge in the small town of Coalinga. Oppressive heat engulfed me as I stepped outside to plug in to the electric. I looked forward to the cool damp air on the coast.

Back inside I stretched out on the couch and tried to unwind. I jumped when my cell buzz-crawled across my desk. Picking it up I saw Margaret's smiling face. She wouldn't be calling if she were mad.

"Maggie! Have you recovered from the move?"

"I want you to come back," she said.

"What? What's wrong? I thought it was okay that I leave?" I took a breath.*What was happening?*

"I thought it would be okay, but it feels like you're abandoning me."

I was. My shoulders slumped. "You said it would be okay...*I felt like I was begging...* if I left ...that we could talk on the phone." I hoped she didn't hear the desperation in my voice. "Has something happened? Do you need something?"

"No. I just don't want you to go."

Her request tore at me. I tried to swallow but couldn't. My poor lost Maggie. She was on her own emotional ride. An unavoidable one with no stops. I wanted to hold her, to take away her fear. But I couldn't. I tried to bargain with the powers above. *Please show me the way.* I'll deal with Michael just make me willing.

"I don't know Maggie," I paced in the small space of my motorhome. I would break if I went home. "I don't think I have anything left to give."

Silence.

I sat back down on the couch and rocked back and forth. "I'll think about it," I finally said.

"Okay." She sounded so far away.

Ending the call, I laid the phone down and stared out the window. Dusty weeds, grew along the fence line. Seeking water in this arid climate, they reached thru the chain link into the graveled RV parking area, in an attempt to encroach onto the pristine black asphalt. My mouth felt as dry and as dusty.

I cleaned up the kitchen and turned down the bed. Spent from curtailing my grief and from damming up the tears, which I refused to cry, I changed into pajamas and crawled atop the cool sheets. Tomorrow I would meet my dear friend, Ashley at the Westport Campground.

CHAPTER TWENTY- EIGHT
2015

I waved as Ashley rolled into the campground and eased her rig past my campsite. I could hear Tika's muffled barking inside Ashley's motorhome. Tika was Ashley's little miniature pincher dog. Energized by her excitement to see me, the little dog bounced up and down on the passenger seat.

After parking two campsites down from me, Ashley swung open her door and Tika's shrill barking mixed with the caws and screes from the gulls.

"Shut up, Tika!" The pup's yapping didn't miss a beat. "Tika, stop!" Tugging at her leash in an effort to greet me the little dog's barking only intensified as they rounded her rig. Ashley giggled. "She's always so excited to see you. She isn't like this with anybody else."

Tika bounced like a basketball. I ignored her antics until she calmed and then bent down to pet her. "I guess we've traveled so much together, she considers Marmalade and me as family." I said. I hugged Ashley. "I've been looking forward to this trip. Boy, do I need it."

"Boy, I need it too. I'm seeing so many changes in Bob, He's forgetting things a lot. He's just not as sharp as he used to be. And now he's talking about selling his racing boats. And then there's a problem with my alcoholic daughter. That's a whole other story." Ashley glanced down at Tika. Her excitement spent, she sniffed around the area her leash would allow. "I've gotta take her for her walk. You want to walk down to the beach?"

I followed behind as Tika led Ashley down the steps to the beach and tide pools. At the bottom of the steps, Ashley squatted and grabbed at a stick, which her little headstrong dog had begun to chew.

"Geeze. She eats everything." She tried to pry the prize from her darling's jaws. Tika growled. "You want a cookie?" Ashley said. Tika released the stick and Ashley tossed it across the beach.

I sat on a rock by the tide pools while Ashley and Tika walked the beach. Run off from Howard Creek gurgled over the stepping stones. A logging truck on Highway One, humming southward and disappeared around the curve. I thought of family cross country road trips on Route 66 when I was a kid and the nights Dad camped under a roadside shade tree. In the darkness, Margaret and I cuddled in bed, listening to the truckers' tires singing as they swooshed by, on their way to some exotic destination, a memory I shared with no one else but my sister.

Ashley returned with Tika and sat down beside me. "How was the drive? Any problems?"

"No driving problems." I brought my knees up to my chest and hugged them as I studied the water gurgling on its way to merge with the ocean.

She glanced over at me. "How's your sister?"

"She called me yesterday afternoon right after I got to Coalinga." I hesitated. Talking about it made it real.

Ashley looked at me and waiting for me to go on. "She wants me to come back."

"Oh boy. Big guilt trip." Ashley picked up a pebble and rolled it around in her palm. "Nothing like digging the blade in all the way." She tossed the stone into the creek.. "Well, you're here, so does that mean you aren't going back?"

"I told her I didn't think I have any more to give."

"And?"

My stomach cramped up again. I wrapped my arms around me and rocked. "In her own way she was saying she needed me not to just to be there, but as a sister." Tears welled up in my eyes and I swiped them with the back of my hand. "I told her I'd think about it."

Ashley stared into the tidepool, tossing another stone into the water. "Well, this is a good place to do that."

"I'm not going back. I can't." I stood up. "I know. You think I am a terrible person." I pushed my shoulders back. "My stomach cramps just thinking about going back. I would have to deal with Michael on his turf. If he says anything to me, I don't know how I could keep from laying into him. I don't want to do that."

Absorbed watching the rippling creek, Ashley said, "I don't see how you've contained yourself this long. I couldn't have kept my mouth shut. I would have told him he's a passive-aggressive lazy shit. It's his mother for God's sake! They shouldn't be laying all the responsibility on her sixty-nine-year-old sister."

"It doesn't matter. I've been judged before." I stood up. Taking a solid stance, I grimaced and raised my chin as I gazed across the ocean at the horizon. "All I know is I'm not going back." I looked down at my friend and forced a big smile. "And for now,I'm going to take a walk, take some pictures and enjoy this beautiful sunset.

CHAPTER TWENTY-NINE
2015

The next morning I awoke to the ocean's steady breathing. I scooted up against the headboard and gazed outside. Marmalade climbed up onto the pillows beside me so he could look out the window, too. Like the Lion King, he laid down, arched his neck at a regal angle, and crossed his front paws. Mesmerized by the powerful heartbeat of the sea, we both contemplated our vast, coastal world.

The fog had crept in during the night on little cat paws, muting the beach noises and silencing the surf. I thought of quiet, snowy mornings from my youth. I didn't have to peer out my bedroom window to know if it had snowed overnight, because the new fallen snow had decorated my world with a magical hush.

Ashley and I were the only ones in the campground. Slipping out of bed, I wriggled into my jeans, and shrugged into my favorite authorial, Mark Twain t-shirt. The rag of a shirt, stretched thin and sagged at the neckline, sharing Twain's purported philosophy printed on the front. "*Be good and you'll be lonely.*" Pulling on a sweatshirt, Ater fixing a cup of coffee I stepped out into the damp air. At the cliff's edge I savored the aroma and warmth from the steaming caffeine.

Three spaces down, Tika's sharp yapping pushed through the fog when Ashley flung open her motorhome door. Clutching a leash in one hand and coffee in the other, Ashley struggled to pull her knit cap down over her ears. Clamoring out of her rig behind Tika, she headed for the beach.

I waved. "Wait up. I 'll walk with you."

Tika led Ashley willy nilly around the campground, seeking out the myriad of beach scents clinging to the grassy scrub. Sniffing and scratching, the little dog poked her nose into a neighborhood of gopher holes dotting our path.

I caught up with the duo as they descended the steps, leading to the beach. We took a leisurely pace toward the tide pools and sat down on a large boulder nearby. Watching the surf in its endless chore of sweeping the beach, I sipped my coffee as Tika busied herself, examining each seashell and every length of twisted driftwood or slimy seaweed.

"Do you think I should go back?" I asked.

Ashley turned to me and put her hand on her hip. "And who then would I travel with up the coast if you do?"

I tried to smile at her teasing. She was very capable of traveling alone.

I squinted, trying to see the horizon through the fog. "I laid awake half the night thinking about what everyone must think of me. Not only did I abandon Margaret, but I also dumped Charlotte on their doorstep, too. It seems I have developed a habit of dropping my loved ones off "like hot potatoes onto their doorstep" ….as Michael puts it."

Ashley tugged on Tika's lead. "No Tika! No! Yuck, she's got a dead bird!" Pulling her pet up close to her, Ashley attempted to yank the carcass from Tika's jaws. The little dog growled.

"Cookie. Cookie!"

Tika dropped the corpse on the sand in anticipation of the promised cookie. Ashley snatched the bird up and tossed it out of the dog's reach.

"Margaret isn't your responsibility." She said as she fed Tika her cookie.

"But Margaret didn't want to go to Michael's house," I countered.

"She didn't have to. She's an adult." Ashley said.

I hung my head. She was right. Margaret could have remained in her house and hired a caregiver. "But still." I said. Like a telemarketer, I couldn't stop arguing my case. "I didn't even rescue my Jeremy and Julia from Charlotte's drug-infested environment. I should have done something."

"You called CPS." Ashley picked up a handful of pebbles and tossed them one by one into the tide pools. "If I remember you told me that's why she quit talking to you."

"I know that was when she cut me off. I didn't hear from her until years later when the girls were about nine and eleven. She reached out to me when she was in a recovery program."

"She was getting sober?"

"Yes, she was so proud of herself. She was going to computer school and she and her boyfriend that she met at a 12-step program were living in a house he owned."

"That was all good right?"

"Yes, I guess it was. The courts gave her the choice of rehab or jail. Of course she chose rehab. I was judgmental and full of distrust. Her housekeeping didn't meet my standards. Little Jasmine pointed to something on the carpet. "Be careful," she said. "That's where the cat threw up."

A pizza box with one dried up piece of pizza was the only food in the refrigerator and a coffee decanter stained black from burnt coffee sat on the stove.

Charlotte asked me to go to court and testify on her behalf so she could get custody of her girls back from her mother-in -law. If she won custody, she would receive more money from welfare.

Like I said, I was judgmental and distrusting. I didn't think she should have custody. I refused. I decided she had only contacted me to make nice, so I would testify and she could win her court case. After I refused, I never heard from her again. Which, at the time, was fine with me. I figured she had tried to use me. The hurt from the emotional ride and the dashed hopes made me swear to myself that I would hang up on her if she ever called me again. I couldn't take all the hurt and disappointment. Obviously, she felt the same.

"I went through that exact same thing with my oldest daughter," Ashley said. "I raised her boys for three years before she finally straightened out.

"At least you tried," I said. "Charlotte would never have allowed me to take her daughters without a custody battle."

Ashley stood. "I'm going to head back. I need some breakfast." She headed down the beah toward toward the steps leading up to the campground. Picking up a stick, I followed, dragging it through the sand.

"I always figured Charlotte would have contacted me if she were sober," I said. "But I should have had more faith in her back then. I should have believed in her. She's gotta be so angry and hurt even if she is sober. I doubt if she will ever forgive me. It's been sixteen years." I said. "Anyway, she's not on Facebook, I've looked. She might be dead.....or brain dead."

We made our way back to the campground the ocean breathed steadily as the waves rushed in and then receded. The endless rhythm pulsed, the sound became hypnotic.

My mind, searching for more guilt subjects found them in the memories of my second marriage. More guilt. More regrets. Rubbing my arms, I kept my head down, feigning attention to the designs my stick created in the sand.

I rarely talked about the marriage with anyone except Margaret. I am still ashamed, so much that I never mention his name.

I had married him because I thought he would be a great father figure, but after five years, I filed for divorce. Something had niggled at me the entire marriage, but I couldn't put my finger on what was wrong. I just knew I was not happy.

One day,he verbally attacked me over a matter with our plumbing business.

"Why didn't you answer the phone?" He was yelling and implying that I had been sluffing off. His habit was to accuse me jump when he was having a bad day. But this time I had enough and I told him so. I had just returned from spending a month in Illinois with Margaret, settling our mother's estate. A month's absence from his dominating attitude made my return annoying and unbearable. I snapped back in retaliation. I yelled, "It was busy!"

He slapped me across the face.

He and I stood face to face. He saw the surprise in my eyes. I had never crossed him. And then I watched the surprise in his eyes as my confusion turned to rage. I said nothing but stood taller. My fists balled up at my side. He saw the challenge in my eyes and dropped his angry stare. With a deceiving calmness,I turned and walked away.

The next morning at 9am I sat in the divorce attorney's office. By afternoon, I had rented a one-bedroom apartment in a not so upscale neighborhood. By nightfall I scooped up our belongings, crammed them into the back of my station wagon and drove away with Charlotte, clutching her stuffed bunny. I left the two-thousand square foot tri-level home in the prestigious Poppy Hill neighborhood and didn't look back. I gave up the full bar with smoked mirrors and the large window with a picturesque view overlooking the valley. I gave up the pool and horse corrals and barn, along with the maid, the gardener and the pool man, And then sued him for everything I could.

As I unloaded our belongings from the car I told Charlotte, "It's just you and me against the world."

That night as she curled up beside me, nestled under my arm Charlotte told me he had been molesting her. She was only eleven.

My heart felt as if it had broken. I didn't know what to say. This was my fault. I was devastated. I hugged her closer to me, "It's okay now, baby. You're safe."

As I look back, I should have done more. I should

have at least talked to her. I should have cut his dick off. Instead, I never talked about it again.

"Things are different now. Ashley said. "You're not the girl you were then."

CHAPTER THIRTY
2015

When I wasn't writing, I spent the time sitting on the beach, digging my toes into the sand and rocking to the sea's rhythmic breathing as the gulls danced on the clean swept shore.

As the days passed, the sea carried away the tension of city life, the angry honks, the abrasive shouts and the choking fumes.

At sunset on the third day Ashley and I made our usual trek down to the waterfront. "Have you had enough of Westport?" She asked. "I thought we could make our next stop Eureka, unless something else draws our fancy."

In the horizon another evening light show had begun. "It's so peaceful here," I said, "but yes, I'm ready to move on."

We retreated to our RVs, lost in our own thoughts. After Ashley and Tikka retired to their rig, I remained outside, watching the last sliver of daylight flicker and go out. The primitive campground faded to black, no street lights, no campfires, only the moon, like a lighthouse, lighting the way.

My mind time-traveled back to my hometown. I thought of the warm Midwestern nights I had shared with Maggie, chasing the magic fireflies of our youth. The reality struck me. When she was gone there would be no one else to whom I could say, "Remember when?" Was I really going to continue on, distancing myself further from Maggie? For the first time I wasn't sure.

The next morning the sun hung over Highway One while the moon made its descent and sank into sea. I grabbed a cup of coffee and trekked out to the cliff to meet the new day.

A thin haze clung to the edge of the cliff as if afraid of heights. The fog, blurred the vista as Kenny Chesney's voice sang, *While He Still Knows who I am*, into my ear buds, creating a mystical mood.

I'm going back to see him, While he still knows who I am......I only knew him as my father ...I'm gonna get to know the man...... I'm gonna kiss him ....I'm gonna tell him that I love him, while he still know who I am.

I had listened to the song many times, but this time the song touched me. On the beach below, the waves pounded out a hypnotic beat. The essence of the place stirred me. A desperate need to hold Maggie's hand swept over me. Tossing the last dregs of my coffee, I pivoted around and strode over to Ashley's rig.

"Ashley." I called thru the screen door. Tika began her incessant barking.

She answered from somewhere in the depths of the motorhome. "Come on in."

climbed the steps and stood in the kitchen. Tika greeted me with her usual rambunctious greeting, dancing around my legs. Ashley bent over the sink washing dishes. Pushing my shoulders back, I rubbed my palms on my thighs, not to warm them, but to calm my nerves.

Ashley glanced up from her chore. "Good mor......."

"I'm going back."

She raised her brows and smiled at me.. I swallowed hard. She probably wondered how many times I was going to change my mind. Outside, the fog had lifted. I wrung my hands. "Suddenly it feels right," I said. I couldn't believe what I was saying. Four days ago I was never going back.

"What made you change your mind?"

"A Kenny Chesney song about a son going back home to visit his father who's suffering from dementia tipped the scale. The lyrics struck a chord. Now I can't get back fast enough." A floodgate of tears opened up and I swiped at my face with my sweatshirt sleeve.

Ashley grinned. "I knew you would."

"You did? How?"

"I just knew."

I put my hand on my hip and gave her a lop-sided grin. "You could have told me. What if I didn't go back? What would you have thought of me then?"

"I knew you were going to. You just needed to de-stress."

"I was burnt out, wasn't I?" I shot her a grateful smile, stepped up to her and hugged her tightly. "Thanks for listening, for being there, for everything." My tears flowing freely again.

 She had had an 'aw shucks' and uncomfortable with my praise, she wanted to busy herself with her dish washing chores, but I held her firmly. "I couldn't have gotten through this without you. Because of you I'm going to be okay, Sis. I love you."

Like I said, I knew you'd figure it out."

Within the hour I was loaded up and ready go, but before I did, I called Maggie.

I'm coming back."

For a moment, only dead air met my ear from Maggie's end of the line. And then, "Wonderful," she said, her voice weak.

I imagined her crying if she had any tears left.

"I should be there tomorrow. I love you, Maggie."

"I love you, too," she said.

I pulled out on the highway to begin the last phase of this death watch.

CHAPTER THIRTY-ONE
2015

Patches of the blue Pacific waved me on as I weaved south on Route 101. I crept into LA with the rest of the traffic. A billboard at the Burbank exit displayed 101 degrees.

The acceptance of my decision to return brought me peace. No more doubts or confusion. I only wanted to hug my dear Maggie and tell her that I loved her. She was my blood, my history, a part of me and I knew there was no time left.

I drove to Michael's. At his driveway gate he buzzed me in and said, "You're here already? The front door's unlocked, so just come on in when you get up to the house. I've got a bad cold so you might want to keep your distance from me."

The gate rolled open.

I stepped through the front door. Shep, Michael's Aussie dog bounded up, his butt waggling. A TV played softly in a bedroom off the den. Michael, his hair unkempt, was stretched out in his pajamas on the u-shaped leather couch, which faced a massive sandstone fireplace. Slider glass doors led to the patio outside. He didn't bother to get up.

Outside on the patio, cardboard boxes had been piled precariously high on top of a handcrafted long oak picnic table. Planks of different lengths of unused lumber leaned against a bamboo fence. Unkempt grass and weeds invaded the spaces between the patio tiles.

I wondered if they had gotten rid of the cat. The hybrid Savanah cat was nowhere to be seen. I had heard the stories of how the thirty-pound cat had attacked Daniel's daughter when his family visited from the east coast. Michael's wife, Tonya, claimed it was an accident, the cat was only playing. Simon, who always believed his opinion was always the right opinion, embraced the camp that the cat was too unpredictable to co-exist with Michael's two-year-old. Simon also mentioned that *IF child services heard of the attack* they would insist the cat be removed. Michael and his camp, including Margaret, interpreted his statement as a threat and only deepened the riff between father and son. Even though Michael leaned toward casting the cat out, he couldn't go against his wife. So they kept the poor animal locked up in a bedroom except when the child was in day care.

Michael popped his head up over the back of the couch. "Mom told me you were coming and said if you just visited every other weekend, it would be okay. Gus wants to visit so he can visit the other weekend." Relief took my tension down a notch. Margaret wasn't expecting me to camp out on Michael's property. I would have, but glad she wasn't asking that of me. I doubt if I were welcomed by Michael, not that he was going to take over Maggie's care. He had moved his mother-in-law from Florida to live in the guest house and take over my job and act as a nanny for the baby. "You can go on in," he said.

I sent him a quick nod and tip toed into the bedroom. Only the dim light of the television and the filtered daylight, which crept past the heavy grey drawn curtains, lit the room. Maggie lay in a hospital bed. Her bluish lids covered her sunken eyes.

I steeled myself against the compulsion to flee. Pushing the bedside table away, I slipped in closer. A dank odor triggered sour acid to rise up in my throat. Twisting away, I pinched the bridge of my nose, squeezed my eyes shut and inhaled. I leaned in, and kissing her cheek, I whispered, "Maggie. It's me".

Her eyelids fluttered, opening slightly. I clutched her hands, which were clasped and resting on her chest. She made a weak effort to pull away from my caress. I had heard that at this stage of life everything hurt, even the lightest touch. I released her hands and pulled back. With a monumental effort, she struggled to unlace her fingers and place her palms together. And she clapped.

Her acclaim was soft, soundless. On and on she clapped. Her eyes remained closed and my tears flowed freely. The room erupted with a luminescence. I wondered if any one witnessed it, or was it only my imagination.

They were the claps of a mime. They said volumes. Maggie's praise, resounded in my heart, like church bells on a Sunday morning. They sang and sobbed, promised and pealed with acclamation.

In all reality, she clapped only once or twice, but no applause had ever meant more to me. I wondered if that was the Grieving Gift, because her performance gave me peace.

CHAPTER THIRTY-TWO
2015

I lay down next to Maggie and took her hand. She squeezed it ever so slightly. My heart burst with the sentiment.

I rolled over, facing her. "I know. You want me to tell you a story."

Throughout her long, bedridden months, too weak to do anything and too strong to give up, she had asked for stories to distract her from her miserable life. "How did your day go?" she would ask. "Tell me what happened with the employee who didn't show up yesterday. Did she come to work today? She wanted to hear about the people I met, and the places I had been, even if it was only a trip to the grocery store.

I had to dig deep to bring up a story. All I could conjure up were the ugly stories that raged and roiled inside my head. The Worry Story: Was my Maggie afraid? What was my future going to be like? The Lonely Story: Would she be alone? No one really knows. Would she worry about me? The Afraid Story: How was I going to make it without her?

I brightened. "Okay I've got a story for you." I smiled over at her. She didn't return the smile but a softness lit up in her eyes.

"Once upon a time there were two widowed sisters," I said. "Neither one had remarried. Their children were grown, living far away, with busy lives of their own. So the sisters talked every day, sharing their secrets and their dreams. They grew very close. They became more than sisters, they became best friends.

"One day one of the sisters fell ill and the doctor informed her she did not have long to live. 'Oh no!' said the healthy younger sister. 'What will I do? I will have no one. Who will I talk to? Who will I go to dinner with or go shopping with? Who will give me a helping hand when I need one?"

"'You should get married again.' The dying woman advised her distressed sibling and best friend.

"Maybe so," the younger woman said. "But who? My dear husband has been gone for years. He was the love of my life. I don't think there's anybody else for me," the devoted sister said.

"There's someone out there for you. I know there is," the sick woman said. "You just have to believe."

The healthy sibling just shook her head and flicked a piece of lint from the bedspread.

The ailing sister pondered for a long moment. "I know! You don't have to worry. I will find someone for you and send him to you. He will be my Grieving Gift to you. Then you will know I am okay and I am always thinking of you." Feeling better about leaving behind her best friend and sister, the dying sister smiled and hugged her sibling.

The healthy sister only laughed at her sister's silliness.

The sad day came when the ailing sister had to say good bye to her loyal sibling. The very next day a handsome gentleman knocked on the grieving woman's door and introduced himself. Tanned and in fine fitting jeans he announced he lived down the street and had heard the sorrowful news about her sister. 'If you need anything, please let me help you,' he said. And, of course, they ended up living happily ever after."

I flopped back on the pillows, delighted with my storybook ending. The slightest of a smile crossed Maggie's dry lips.

"And don't forget," I said to Maggie. "Just like the old widow story, you're going to send me a Grieving Gift, too. I expect him to be wearing fine fitting jeans."

CHAPTER THIRTY- THREE
2015

G lad to be alone with my thoughts and away from Maggie's reality, I settled back in the driver's seat, and took a few deep breaths. The L.A. traffic report described the east bound lanes as light, but in this hick town girl's opinion, I had never seen "light traffic" in L.A.

Before I left, Michael went over Margaret's care with me. He and Margaret were happy with the quality of care from LA's hospice doctors and nurses. His mother-in-law monitored Margaret's medications efficiently and Margaret's long-time L.A. friends and family, who all had busy, important lives, now took time to visit and comfort her. According to Michael,

Margaret was on the magical L.A. carpet ride to heaven.

Months before, Maggie shared with me that she considered the mother in law irritating, uneducated and inept. It had been a long time since she welcomed visits from friends. It required too much effort. She just wanted to be left alone, but of course, she never would say anything. She would lie before she would ever risk hurting someone's feelings.

The words of my friend, Ashley, who had worked as a hospice volunteer came forefront in my mind. "There were never any earth-shaking revelations or transformations in people's lives when they are on their death beds. That only occurs in the movies." she had explained. "People die the way they've lived."

During my visit two weeks later, Maggie was more lucid. I stretched out beside her. A scenic vistas with horses grazing in a lush green pasture appeared on the TV screen.

"I wish I lived there," Maggie said.

Surprised, I gazed over at her. Not once since we were eight year old, stealing tomatoes in the night from the neighbor's garden , had I ever heard Maggie dream of anything that didn't have a huge price tag on it. I took her hand and held it. "Me too," I said. I thought it strange for Maggie, who had lived in one of the poshest neighborhoods in L.A.to make such a statement.

During the next several visits conversation was minimal, most of the time she slept. My visits became shorter and shorter as the ache of losing Maggie grew larger, and the ninety-mile trek back and forth grew longer.

The drive into the city, which used to be only an unpleasant chore, now became agonizing and urgent. The intense pull of longing to see Maggie just one more time gave me the strength and yet, as soon as I arrived I longed to distance myself from the sadness, which I couldn't escape.

The drive home couldn't be short enough, yet it was long enough to remind me that this may be the last drive home.

CHAPTER THIRTY-FOUR
2015

I t was Gus's week to visit Maggie so I joined several RV friends for the weekend at a nearby camp out.

Since before daybreak, I spent the early October morning hunched over my laptop pounding out the rough draft of my next chapter. When the sun chased away the night sky, I stood up and stretched, taking a moment to enjoy the transition of a new day. I wondered if Margaret was still fighting for one more day when my cell began to flash and vibrate as if ready to answer my unspoken question. I stared down at Michael's face on the screen. The sun ceased its ascent. Drawing in a deep breath, I braced myself and clicked the answer button.

"Michael?"

"Mom passed away peacefully last night."

 I had expected the call. But still, the sad news hit like a sucker punch, sending me to my knees. A door slammed shut.

I was now officially on my own. My Maggie, my sister, my best friend was gone. I begged the universe to reassure me she was okay on her new journey. She had struggled so.

My world shrank to one dimension. Staring out into the dead air in the campground, I think I mumbled a thank you to Michael. I don't remember.

I didn't move. If I remained in a suspended stupor, I hoped to be invisible to the hurt and pain waiting to rush in. The somber stillness changed the colors of the vista outside to a storm cloud grey and the sky to an ice cold blue.

When one door shuts another one opens. That's what everyone says. I shouted out. "Fuck the Pollyanna attitude." I was done opening doors.

I cried. This time for me. I didn't feel so tough. Studying my new barren world outside, I tried to turn my heart to stone. I don't remember the day passing. Finally, darkness slugged onto the stage. The setting faded to a joyless black with no breeze. I don't know how long I sat comatose, but frigid air forced me to get up. I stumbled around my rig, closed the door, the windows and pulled the shades.

That felt better.

I was eight years old again, hiding in my bedroom closet, safe from a scary world I didn't want to face. The campground street lights flickered on and I crawled off to bed.

In the morning, consciousness jarred me awake. Before I could slam the floodgate shut, reality rushed in.

I dragged myself from bed, made a cup of coffee and called Ashley. She said the things that people do. "She's at rest now. She's free to soar, and so are you."

"I don't feel much like soaring."

"You got back in time. That's good," she said. "She was waiting for you."

I described to Ashley how Maggie applauded when she saw me.

"You see? I told you." Ashley's cheery voice irritated me. "People decide when it is time to go," she said. "Are they going to have a memorial service?"

"I didn't ask. If they do, I won't go. During all this time no one offered their sympathies to me. I doubt if they will now."

The thought of having to make nice one more second with the condescending family caused the acid in my stomach to churn. The image of the high school principal's secretary handing me my diploma, popped into my mind's eye. I tossed the phone down and yelled into it. "Hold on!"

I charged into the bathroom. When the heaving subsided, I rinsed out my mouth and picked the phone back up. "Sorry. You still there? I threw up."

"Wow. You really don't like those people."

"It is more than that. Until now, I never had the opportunity to get to know them so intimately. They believe they're superior to others because of their intellect, social status and wealth. Their elitist attitude. I can't bear it."

I choked back the bile rising in my throat.

"Anyway, Margaret said she didn't care about a service, but I think the boys will want one."

"Are you going to take off now? You're free, girlfriend! You can go anywhere."

"Yes, that part feels wonderful, but now don't you think it's getting too chilly to head up the coast? "

"It is. Hey! Why don't you go to Death Valley Days with me? It will be fun."

"I've been wanting to attend that for years. That sounds like a plan." Ashley threw out the dates and I penciled them in on my calendar. And just like that, my new reality began.

Cheered somewhat, after talking to Ashley, I posted the news of Margaret's death on Facebook. Because of my author status I had acquired a considerable amount of fans who follow me. My cell began dinging with dozens of notifications from my readers, posting their prayers and sympathies.

I scrolled through the comments, responding to well-wishers, from all over the country and Europe. Many of them I have never met, but I have come to know on Facebook since my writing career began to blossom. I paused at a name I did not recognize. But one that struck a familiar chord. Brent Dickerson. He had messaged me about six months ago when I announced Margaret had gone on hospice. I remembered his strange comment, *"Mom, what is wrong Aunt Margaret?"*

I had no son named Brent. The message had creeped me out. I disregarded it as someone who had me confused with someone else or a scammer.

Now he was messaging me again. *"Mom. Could you please tell me what happened to Aunt Margaret?"*

I felt sorry for the guy. He must have me confused with someone else. He needed to know this Aunt Margaret was not his Aunt Margaret. I messaged him back. *"I don't know who you are, but you have me confused with someone else. I am not your mother."*

The mystery reminded me that I had promised myself to search for Charlotte. I had no expectations of a happy ending when I found her or even if I could find her, but the urgency to make my amends to her weighed on me. Finding her would be the top priority in my new future.

Facebook dinged again. Brent had replied.

"Mom, this is your daughter, Charlotte."

CHAPTER THIRTY- FIVE
2015

I stared at the screen, rereading the words. I clicked on Brent's profile. The people sitting at restaurant table were strangers.

But wait.

I ran the numbers in my head. Charlotte would be in her fifties, not sixteen. I studied the family, smiling up at the camera from a restaurant booth, and zeroed in on one woman with shoulder length hair. She had Charlotte's smile— my smile.

I clicked back and read the message again. My pulse raced, afraid to hope. I fumbled with my phone as I pecked out a response. *I have thought about you so many times.*

Me, too.

Oh my God!! I didn't know that Brent Dickerson was you! I would have answered you back when you messaged me, six months ago! I am so sorry! How are you?

"Brent's my husband. We've been married twelve years. You met him the last time I saw you." She typed in her phone number and said, *"Call me"*.

Aaaah, I remember, the boyfriend! My hands trembled. I dropped the phone. Fumbling it, I dropped it again. At last, I punched in the numbers. It took several times before I got it right.

"Hello," Charlotte's soft voice was like a rich new melody.

"I have thought of you often," I said, fighting for air.

"Me too. I've grown up a lot.

I smiled at the irony. "I have too," I said. "I've missed you terribly."

"Me too, Mom."

Mom? There was no stopping them now. The tears gushed down my face. I never thought I'd hear her call me that ever again. The reality of what was happening struck me. *Don't screw this up, Janice.*

"We're living in the same place in San Bernardino, but the house burnt down in the Fire Siege of 2003. We rebuilt on that same lot".

She went on. *"Besides, Julia and Jasmine you also have two great grandsons. I'm the secretary to the San Bernardino County Board of Supervisors. I've worked there fifteen years."*

This is my baby. She's all grown up. She's such an adult. Her babies have babies of their own.

"I'm so proud for you." Somehow I choked back a lifetime of sobs.

So what happened to Aunt Margaret?

I caught her up on the details of Margaret's illness. "The memorial service will be next week," I said. "It will probably be at Michael's house. Would you like to go? "

"Yes I would."

"I wasn't going to attend, but if you go, I will."

I didn't want to go alone and I guessed she didn't either. Charlotte had lived with Margaret and Simon for two years after she turned sixteen. Now, that I had learned so much about the family I wondered what it had been like for her

"Maybe we could get together before the memorial service? I would love to see you." I didn't want my first time seeing Charlotte to be at the memorial service and certainly didn't want to share the miracle moment with those people."

"We have a birthday party Saturday, so maybe Monday?"

"A birthday party?"

"It's for your great grandson, Justin. Would you like to come?"

Oh my God! She's inviting me to her home to meet her family. My family. The tears which had receded now spewed forth again, this time driven by excitement and fear. Everything was happening so fast. I drew up my courage. "I would love to."

"I'll text you the address. But I don't want you saying anything about my messy house."

"Are you kidding? I don't care about your house. All I have ever wanted was for you to have a good life." I was glad she couldn't see me crying. "What time?"

After our good byes, I sat, stunned, trying to make sense of this incredulous moment. My sister, who had believed that when you are dead you are dead had had a hand in this. I had no doubts. THIS was my Grieving Gift.

The forty-nine mile drive to Charlotte's house would take sixty minutes if there were no backups on the freeway. I gave myself ninety.

When I thought of Margaret, the sadness overcame me, but just as quickly, my mind turned to Charlotte's appearance, an event which I had long ago given up hope of ever happening.

I wouldn't be making this drive if Charlotte had not forgiven me for all l the mistakes I had made, for all the times I had hurt her, and for the times I put her in harms way and didn't protect her.

When I climbed in the car to make this life changing drive I swore I would not let the years of guilt erupt and make this meeting all about me. I am not sixteen anymore, I am not that opinionated, self-centered woman who has all the answers.

As I maneuvered onto the freeway, I swiped away the tears which I couldn't control no matter how hard I tried. Traffic was heavy. I couldn't pull over. I couldn't fall apart. I couldn't be late.

CHAPTER THIRTY-SIX
2015

I shoved fifty years of guilt, remorse and should haves, would haves and could haves to the back seat and focused on arriving on time. I would be making the most important entrance of my life, into a house full of strangers I didn't know, but who surely knew my darkest secrets.

Charlotte told me to be there about two. To me that meant sharply at two. The GPS displayed the present time, one-thirty. So far traffic moved at a pretty good clip. "It is twenty miles to your destination," the device announced. "Your arrival time is one-fifty." Ten minutes ahead of schedule.

Red lights! I slammed on the brakes. Taillights lit up all lanes. I gripped the wheel even harder as California's life rolled to a standstill at the 60 and 215 interchange. I kept glancing at the time. One forty-three. I can't be late. I could not have Charlotte think for one moment that I was not coming. My mind searched for an alternative route while my eyes darted back and forth trying to peer past the artery of cars and the clot at the interchange. One forty-five.

Inside my head, the few minutes turned into an hour. One-forty-six. Glory be! The taillights blinked out. California took a slow breath, then another. Creeping up to speed, the traffic returned to its regular eighty miles per hour heartbeat. I prayed for a healthy pace the rest of the way.

A smile spread across my face. The traffic panic attack had taken my mind off the emotional moment which I would be facing in exactly — I checked the GPS — fifteen miles, estimated arrival time, two o'clock.

As I pulled up to the curb. I checked the time., One-fifty-nine! Perfect!

One of the worst flash fires in the county had swept through Charlotte's neighborhood in 2003, randomly taking out houses. Hers had been one of many homes peppered throughout that had been reduced to its charred foundation. Now rebuilt, it stood apart from its elders in a defiant glory.

A hulking Ford Explorer parked in the driveway made me smile. Why did I expect a piece-of-shit car? She had already told me she had been working fifteen years as the secretary for the county board of supervisors. I was glad she didn't drive a Prius. In L.A. everyone who didn't lease a Tesla or a Maserati drove a Prius. Not that there was anything wrong with a Prius, but I couldn't separate my newly developed L.A.prejudice from the car. Charlotte and her family had chosen common sense and roominess.

Charlotte and her husband, Brent came out the front door. They met me as I made my way half-way up the walkway. She wore a Snoopy T-shirt and capris, while Brent was casual, too, in sweats and a T-shirt. Both carried extra pounds, which they told me later motivated them to join L.A. Fitness.

Charlotte had twisted her shoulder length hair and pinned it on top of her head. Her prominent cheekbones and the same azure eyes as mine accented her beauty. My little girl was a looker, as I had always predicted.

The incredibility increased with each step as I approached this piece of my heart which I had had given to my higher power so many, many years ago for safe keeping. I don't remember breathing. I was suspended in time, an astonished stranger, looking down on an unbelievable, unimaginable moment. I had long ago abandoned even dreaming about this moment.

These last steps, became a lifetime. Every argument, every broken heart moment, every night when I cried myself to sleep wishing I had been a better person, all those times I bargained with God, on my knees, begging him to take care of her, of hating myself, of wondering if she were dead…. Like puffs of smoke, it all dissipated into the air between us. The misery, the loneliness, regrets and anger vanished.

We wrapped our arms around one another and held onto each other like the other was a lifeline. All the money in L.A. could not have bought me the magic I now felt.

She had forgiven me.

I choked back a sob and she cleared her throat. I loosened my embrace and pulled away before I lost control. She did the same because she is her mother's daughter.

I turned to Brent and we shook hands. "How was the drive?" he asked, trying to find some kind of normalcy to this miracle.

"Pretty good," I said as I glanced up at their home "You have a nice place. Charlotte tells me you guys did a lot of the rebuilding yourselves."

"We did. The mortgage is paid off, too," Charlotte said. Her confidence and pride made me want to burst with my own pride. .

"I remember when it was like the one across the street." I glanced at the original house. It sat far back from the street, leaving a spreading front yard. Charlotte's home spanned the entire lot leaving only a small patch of lawn between the structure and the sidewalk.

Charlotte reached out, placed her hand on my shoulder and guided me toward the front door. "Come on in and meet your great grandsons and everyone else."

CHAPTER THIRTY-SEVEN
2015

We followed the myriad of voices into the kitchen. The spacious kitchen appeared small since it seemed to be the gathering place of my new family. Everyone mingled around a long oak table, munching from plates of vegetable plates and bags of chips bowls of dip. In the adjoining den, children's laughter rang out above the drone of the big screen TV.

Brent leaned in and pecked what I guessed was a reassuring kiss on Charlotte's cheek. "I'll be outside tending to the barbeque." he said. The sound of a basketball's steady thumping filtered inside before the backdoor shut behind him.

Charlotte and I squeezed into the crowded kitchen and she began making introductions — my youngest granddaughter, her husband , both just out of the Army, and their four-year-old, my great-grandson.— Brent's mother, a proper woman of British descent, was gracious and a little flustered that she was meeting, 'a famous author.' — Brent's daughter from a previous marriage and her two eight and nine-year -old sons. — And lastly, my oldest grandson who stole my heart when he sized me up with his intelligent amber eyes.

One day I had no one, and now I have this family, enough to crowd a room. I hoped my nervousness didn't show. I tried to remember how long it had been since I felt so out of place. Yet, everyone was friendly. Their curiosity, their opinions, their judgements, all which I am sure they harbored about me, they kept to themselves. They didn't seem to be bothered by my presence. They laughed and joked amongst themselves in contrast to my nervous reserve.

The menu was simple, hamburgers, hot dogs, chips and store bought potato salad. "Time to chow down," Brent announced as he brought in a platter of meat. Everyone scrambled to find a seat. "Boys you're at the breakfast bar," Charlotte said as she pulled out the stools.

After cake and ice cream, birthday gifts and bedtime kisses, the big house, full of my family, quieted. When all the goodbye hugs and "nice to meet yous" were finished, Charlotte, Brent and I sat at in the kitchen over coffee.

"You have such a lovely family, Charlotte." I smiled at her. "And your home's not messy."

I looked at Brent. "I wanted you to know that I didn't remember you. If I had known I would have responded to your message. I am so sorry. I friend a lot of people whom I don't even know, because of my books. I assumed you were just a fan."

Brent smiled at me then focused his eyes on wife's reaction as he said, "I friended you," he said. "I figured it was time you two got back together."

I stammered, knowing my son-in-law had done this for Charlotte. "I— I —I'm so glad you did."

Charlotte, remained quiet, non-committal. I laid my hand over hers and squeezed it. "I'd already decided that after Margaret was gone that I would search for you. I had asked Margaret if she would like me to try to find you, but she said no. "I don't want to face her," she said to me. She told me she felt as if she had failed you.

Charlotte listened, remaining reserved and non-committal, as if trying to decide how to respond. "I told Margaret that I didn't think she had failed you. At least she got you to graduate high school."

Charlotte smiled. "Yes, she did."

"I always thought you would have contacted me if you had been clean and sober," I said. "So, when you didn't, I thought you were dead or brain-dead. "I leaned back in my chair and grinned. "And look at you now." I motioned to include the surroundings. "For one thing, you have this beautiful home which you guys have managed to pay off. Do you realize how few people these days accomplish that? And there's your long- time employment with a prestigious position. You're incredible." I grinned again. "You've done quite well without this wise old woman's guidance."

My attempt to lighten the subject brought a smile to her face. "Margaret taught me a lot about saving," Charlotte said.

"That's great, I said. " I'm glad you had the opportunity to live with them. I doubt if you would have graduated if you hadn't gone to live there."

Charlotte offered no more response than, "Thanks Mom."

"It's getting late," I said as I rose from the table. I was certainly not going to overstay my welcome. "I'm sure it's been a big day for you, too. It certainly has been for me. I should be heading home, it will be dark soon. I don't like driving in the dark."

Charlotte rose, too. "Thanks for coming, Mom." she said, leaning in to hug me.

"Are you kidding? It was wonderful." We held each other, each not wanting to let go.

"I love you, Mom."

At last we released one another. "I love you too, Charlotte. Thank you so much for having me."

"Do you still want to do lunch?" Charlotte asked. "I'm off this Monday. Brent and I could come by about noon."

"That would be great."

I had made the cut! She wanted to see me again! *One day at a time, Janice.. Just respect her and love her.* I sensed she wanted to talk more. We had sixteen years to catch up on.

CHAPTER THIRTY- EIGHT
2015

I decided on a more intimate setting and fixed lunch at the house so we wouldn't have to go out. When they arrived I gave them the tour of the house. I pointed out the varnished wall clock with the image of the Klaipeda Waterfalls, a gift she had brought back from her graduation trip to Hawaii. She spent time browsing the family photos and her baby pictures hanging in the foyer.

"I remember some of these paintings," she said as she stepped into the last bedroom which I had converted into a gallery of my paintings.. She wandered past each painting, examining the artwork.

"Yes, many of the oils you'll remember. They're some of my best. My newer pieces I don't think are as good. I haven't painted in a long time. I think I am a better writer than I am a painter, but some day, when I have more time, I would like to dabble in it again. "

Brent followed behind his wife. "I think they're all good."

I laughed. "I'm my worst critic."

In my bedroom I opened up my Dad's Navy foot locker in which stored all the mementoes of all our lives — Margaret's, mine and Charlotte's — bronzed baby shoes, and baby teeth and locks of hair. — bracelets, report cards and graduation pictures. Charlotte dropped down on the floor and began sifting through the past. "When we have more time you should sort through these things and take what's important to you," I said.

Charlotte singled out several photos. "I remember this house," she said. She ran her finger over another photo. She was about four and wore a red pinafore dress trimmed in yellow and a red tam o' shatter hat with a bright yellow pom-pom. Clutching a white knitted purse which hung from her shoulder, she squinted up at the camera. "I hated that outfit."

"But look at it. You were so cute." I remember a time when she would have laughed harder at my teasing.

Brent threw an arm around her. "Oh, look, she still is."

"Oh look at this," I said. "A valentine you made and gave to Grandpa." Charlotte smiled

After walking around in the backyard and checking out the motorhome, we sat around the patio table. I served sandwiches and iced tea on the patio.

"Recently we've been discussing our retirement," Brent said. "I'm taking my retirement next year. Charlotte will have a few more years before she's able to." He patted her hand. "We've been playing with the idea of buying a motorhome. But we're looking something bigger than yours."

"That's exciting." I said. "Boy, it's hard to believe I'm sitting here talking to my baby girl about retiring. How cool would that be? I could follow behind you guys in my little rig."

Charlotte, who I was learning was the practical one said, "Yes, but I don't see that happening soon. We're raising Jeremy. He's still in school."

I didn't ask for details. If Charlotte wanted me to know more about Jeremy's mom, she would tell me. For now, she only explained Jasmine's absence as, "Jasmine's busy doing her own thing."

"You could home school Jeremy," I said, with enthusiasm. "I could help."

"We've talked about that, too," Brent said. "But we have time to figure it all out."

A grim expression flashed across Charlotte's face. Whatever Jasmine's thing was, it wasn't good. "So, what did Michael say when you told him I was coming to the memorial?" Charlotte asked.

"Actually, I didn't tell him. I asked him. I wasn't even sure that I was welcome until they actually gave me the date and the location. Michael will be nice to you one minute and then stab you in the back the next minute." I shared the story of Michael's attack on my care giving abilities when he thought I should "make" Margaret eat. "Michael can turn on you in a second."

"I know how they are," Charlotte said. "Remember I lived with them for two years. The entire family treated me like an outsider. When all the family got together for a family affair, Simon's sister would herd my cousins away from me if they started playing with me. They never said anything, they just smiled their phony smiles and then kept me at a distance."

"Really?" I couldn't hide my surprise.

"I got nothing new. If there was something I wanted I had to pay for it with the money I earned working at McDonald's. They gave me hand-me-downs, usually stuff the boys didn't want anymore. I had to pay for my own Kotex."

I could tell she saw the surprise in my eyes. "Really?" I said again. "I believed I was sending you to a stable loving home." I shook my head. A deep sadness came over me. "I told everyone at least you were finally able to experience the stable environment, which I had not been capable of giving you. I couldn't understand why you just walked out when you turned eighteen."

"Well, it was true. And Simon's not the guy you think he is, either. Of course, everyone knows he's a dickhead, but he was a lot worse than that."

She was into her story now. Her breaths short, her words clipped. "He beat me often. Granted, my attitude was bad, but you just don't cross Simon. Ever.

"Many times me and the boys huddled, scared to death in my bedroom with the door closed while he and Margaret had one of their knock-down, drag-out arguments."

She caught a quick breath. "I hated it there. I couldn't wait to turn eighteen and get out."

I sat, across from Charlotte, unmoving, as if I had turned to stone, Her revealing story came easy enough from her lips. I could tell she had spent considerable hours working through the damaging effects of that part of her life.

My world shifted as I sat there, listening to the nightmare my daughter had lived. "I didn't know."

"Well, it's true," she repeated with a tinge of anger.

I jumped up. Rushing around the table, I wrapped my arms around her. My voiced squeaked. "My poor baby. I believe you. I have no doubts."

Hugging her, I squeezed her tightly, kissing her cheek. I took her hand and I held it between mine. "But I'll be honest with you. I doubt if I would have believed you back then if you had told me.

"All these years," I said, "I've clung to that one thin string of redemption, in which I had done one thing right, by sending you to a loving, stable home. And now I learn this?" I hung my head. "I am so, so sorry. I just didn't know.

"It's okay, Mom." She patted my hand.

I took a deep breath and stiffened . I didn't deserve my daughter comforting me.

I pulled away from her and sat back down. "If I had not taken care of Margaret this last year, I'm not so sure I would believe you even today. But I've experienced Michael and Daniel, and even Margaret, switch from sweet and kind to the intense anger like a wounded wild cat. Really scary."

On a death watch sometimes you don't learn thing until they are gone. Never once did my Maggie mention the abuse. She thought she had taken the ugliness with her to her grave.

CHAPTER THIRTY – NINE
2015

I met Charlotte, Brent and Jeremy in the parking lot outside the Burbank Country Club. Brent no longer wore the casual look. His suit sported a buttoned jacket, pleated pants and his oxfords looked new. I already had learned enough about him to know he was Charlotte's rock.

My little family made a united entrance. Michael and Daniel stood at attention beside one another masquerading in their tragedy masks, which hid years of family secrets and disagreements. At the entrance to the Serenity Room they greeted aunts, uncles, cousins and friends of the family. Shakespeare's words from Macbeth came to mind …. *Tis time! Tis time! Round about the cauldron go* …. Months before Margaret's passing new tensions over the estate finances had been mixed into the cauldron. *Double, double toil and trouble* ….

I searched the masquerade, hoping to catch sight of Simon, the one who had once held the reins as the mighty family ruler. I always knew Simon's list of flaws was long and ugly — hard-nosed, opinionated, verbally abusive and crass. Everyone knew exactly where he stood on any matter. No one crossed him. But now after all what Charlotte had revealed, I saw him with new eyes.

Simon had not been awarded his throne in the divorce, and it was obvious Michael had stepped up to fill the role.

We found Simon in the Serenity room. He rushed up to me. I hugged him and when I stepped back, his eyes glistened with tears. A man who had always been angry at life, was now a bundle of tight restraint. Simon escorted me to a front row seat with my name on it next to Michael and Daniel. Then he turned to Charlotte, they hugged and exchanged a few pleasantries. He motioned to Charlotte. "Michael assigned you guys to the second row." He coughed in an attempt to cover his emotions, then he told Charlotte, "Michael assigned me to the back row." His voiced cracked. "And he's not letting me speak." If Charlotte noticed him blinking back tears, she didn't react but busied herself getting Jeremy seated.

I would have wondered how anyone could be so cruel to their own father at such a moment, but now I realized the reverberations of Simon's behavior ran deep. It was Michael's turn now. And he was his father's son. He ruled now. No one was crossing Michael today.

Family members trickled past me and my cherished little family, feeding me their 'How have you beens?' and 'Nice to see yous', which I didn't spit out. I suffered through the facade like a badly cooked meal. When called upon to speak, I read my eulogy which I had prepared. My last words to Margaret. I wanted these people to know who my Maggie really was. She was so much more than the part she had played.

"Margaret was my sister. When we were kids I called her Maggie because I knew she found the nickname low class. Yet Margaret clung to my nickname, Turn, short for Turnip. Even in adulthood, and even when I insisted I had outgrown my foolish childhood name long ago. And now, I wish I could hear her call me Turn just one more time.

Did you know our parents lived in childless marriage for sixteen years? So they were surprised and ecstatic when Margaret came into this world. She was their miracle child, and she paved the way for me a year and a half later. I was my mother's child, full of adventure and the rebel. But Margaret took after our father, freckle-faced, serious, and always in control.

As I wrote this eulogy, I recalled a friend's words who consoled me during this difficult time. My friend told me, "We die like we lived."

My sister lived her life to help others. You all knew her kindness and love. And now in death, in this little sister's opinion, my sweet Maggie, who had worried about leaving her little sister alone in the world, has had a hand in bringing my daughter and me back together ...ironically, after sixteen years. Charlotte is Margaret's Grieving Gift to me. "

Charlotte rose from her seat, squeezed past Brent and hurried down the aisle, exiting the Serenity Room.

"Margaret was my best friend, my opposite and she is my miracle maker." I scanned the crowd. "I have no doubt she will continue to help others, and work her miracles for you, too."

I gazed into the empty air above the mourners. *"I want to thank you, Maggie, for my Grieving Gift. You aced it. You will be dearly missed by your little sister."*

I made my way back to my seat, sending a questioning look to Brent because Charlotte had not returned. He whispered into my ear." Your speech made her cry. She may be tough on the surface, but she's a softy."

Just like her mom.

CHAPTER FORTY
2015

As the weeks rolled by, I thought of Maggie often. — A funny post on Facebook, a song on my playlist, or a beautiful flower. — Triggers which reminded me I could no longer share them with her. I often gazed at the newspaper clipping from The Illinois Journal & Register, which Maggie had framed and given me. It hung in my tiny grooming room off the garage. The article reported of better days when we were teens just before everything turned complicated. The Journal & Register praised our teenage entrepreneurship with a half page photo of Maggie and me, scissors poised, grooming a full coated white standard poodle. I remember the dog's name was Panda. These flashbacks came often, memories in which there is no one else to whom I can say, "Remember when?" Only my Maggie.

During these moments my heart would begin to weep, but as if a switch had been pushed, the reality of Charlotte's presence in my life swept in and washed away my grief. It was magic. By the time December approached I realized it was impossible to grieve for Maggie, I could only rejoice for the Gift she had given me.

Life began to become routine, as if that wasn't a miracle in itself? To be routine when I am meeting my family for Sunday brunch, a family whom I had no idea even existed? We talked of Christmas presents and Christmas dinner.

Throughout my death watch, I rarely missed a meeting with my writing critique group. My writing and my author friends were the two constants I clung to that carried me through the emotional ride. Over the years my fellow writers, like family, witnessed me and my writing at my best, and at my worst They held my hand, whispering words of encouragement when I believed my loss was too much to bear. And they cheered in amazement when Charlotte came into my life, many never knowing I had a daughter.

On December 2, 2015 my writers group had wrapped up another great critiquing session and I headed out to my car. As was my style, I was always in a rush to complete my errands so I could return home and finish the edits which had been suggested.

Looking back, December 2nd has fallen into that same category as other dates that you know you will never forget. Those days when you remember exactly where you were and what you were doing. December 2nd was like one of those days. — Like the day when Kennedy was shot, or the day I received the call that my mother had died, or like 9-11. December 2nd was also my Maggie's birthday, if she had lived.

I had settled into the driver's seat, and checked my errand list, my email and Facebook notifications. The quiet in the car was rare. I hadn't turned the ignition, so no music blasted from the speakers as it usually did. The sun, beating through the windshield, warmed the interior, although the chilly day called for a jacket. The newsfeed on Facebook rolled past, scrolling on its own as if it were running off at the mouth. *Mass shooting…terrorists….San Bernardino ….*The feed sped across the screen. I didn't want to take time to read it…sadly, shootings were becoming so commonplace*. San Bernardino Regional Medical Center ….14 dead…many wounded…..*

WAIT! I clicked on one of the headlines. San Bernardino Regional Medical Center….. NO! My breathing ceased. The pounding I heard was not a carpenter's hammer, it was my body pumping adrenaline into my veins. I wanted to scream. The rush swished in my ears making it hard to hear.

Charlotte worked at the San Bernardino Regional Medical Center!

Now my breathing came fast, yet I gasped for air. Tears flooded my face. *Maybe I'm wrong. This might not be where she works.* The text blurred. I fumbled the cell phone. It slipped from my sweaty grasp and clattered to the floorboard. My hands trembled and my body shook all over. *NO!* I said again. *She has to be okay!*

Anger took over and seized me with a vengeance. *If I were there I would sink a thousand bullets into every fucking son of a bitch threatening my Charlotte.* There would be no stopping me except a terrorist bullet. I recalled a war story my father had shared with Maggie and me long ago. He had pumped a Japanese soldier full of bullets, emptying his magazine. He told us he carried the guilt of that all his life, not that he had killed the man, but that he had lost control. He promised himself he would never lose control again. I know how he felt. I felt the same rage as my father had. It consumed me with a power I had never experienced. My rage was out of control and I knew I could kill anyone in my way to protect my daughter. I didn't care. I could kill them one hundred times and suffer no guilt.

This might not be where she works. You're not sure. I recovered the phone off the floor and managed to punch in her number through tear-filled eyes.

She picked up on the first ring. "Are you okay?" I asked.

"I'm okay, Mom. We're in the building next door. We're in lockdown. We're safe."

"Oh thank goodness!" I broke out in sobs.

"Mom, mom. It's okay. I'm safe." I heard the tension in her voice.

She was safe. My baby was safe.

After she hung up, I wiped my tears and sucked in deep breaths as I tried to regain some kind of control. My violent reaction surprised me. Less than two months ago I had assumed my daughter was dead or brain dead, or at the very best in God's hands living out her life without me, thank you very much. How could my world have shifted so drastically?

I went to my Facebook page and posted that my daughter worked at the medical site of the terrorist attack. *"Thank God my daughter is safe. After being separated for sixteen years I cannot have something happen to her now."*

Ten minutes later my cell rang, a number I didn't recognize. "Hello."

"Hello, This is Christina from NBC News. We understand your daughter is on scene at the terrorist attack. We're glad she's safe. We have a team flying out to cover the shooting and would like you and your daughter to be on the Today Show in the morning."

"The Today Show?"

"Yes. We think you and your daughter have a unique story to tell."

"Oh." I tried to grasp what was happening. "The Today Show?" I repeated.

They were out for the story. My daughter would have inside information about the attack. I would sell a lot of books. Our sixteen year estrangement and then this. What a story. Hell, I wanted to write it!

"Oh," I said again. "I don't think so." *What?* I heard myself turning down an opportunity to be on The Today Show. A measure of sanity crept into my mind. All they really wanted to know was information about the shootings. Our story would make a good one.

"No?" Like me, Christina couldn't believe I was turning down such an opportunity.

Coming out of shock from the entire ordeal, I repeated more confidently, "No. My daughter has a high security clearance and I am sure she would not be allowed to talk about the shootings." As badly as I wanted the chance to promote my books over national television, I didn't want to do anything that might jeopardize my relationship with Charlotte. It was way too soon for us to talk about our estrangement and our reunion.

The next week at my writing group I relayed the latest drama in my life, my life which, was developing more twists and turns than any Hallmark movie ever written. The moderator of the group and whom I have named as my mentor, shook his head in amazement. "You have to write about this," he said.

I nodded, also overwhelmed by the rapid set of occurrences. "I know."

CHAPTER FORTY-ONE

2015

The morning after the terrorist attack, as I clung to the last moments of warm bed covers and snuggles with Marmalade, my cell buzzed me fully awake. "Good morning, Charlotte," I said. "How're you doing?" I assumed she wanted to talk about the attack.

"I have to fly up to Redwood City. Jasmine is in intensive care. They have to put a stint in her brain."

What?! My little Jasmine whom I took to Disneyland when she was four? The girl who is 'doing her own thing'?

"What happened?

"I've wanted to tell you about her, but it never seemed like the right time."

"What is it, Sweetheart?" I heard the pain in her voice, she was near tears.

"Jasmine's dying. She's in intensive care. She has AIDS, meningitis and valley fever."

"Oh dear." I didn't know what to say. AIDS implies so many things.

"When Jasmine was thirteen, right after I got sober, she kept running away. My life was still a mess. I tried with her, I really did. But she hooked up with the Bloods and the Crypts. And then a girl solicited her and told her she didn't have to live like that. She offered her a better life. Jasmine became a prostitute."

My heart sank. *A prostitute*. The words stuck in my throat. My sweet baby granddaughter with the fiery spirit. The one I didn't fight for custody of. But I didn't have time for guilt now. It would always be there. I shook it off.

The news hit me hard. Bile rose up in my throat. If I never believed in some kind of power in the universe guiding us, I did now. I knew all about prostitutes and sex trafficking. The book I was currently writing, due to be published in a couple of months, touched on the serious issue of sex trafficking.

Out of all the troublesome issues to address in this world, why did I pick one of the ugliest and saddest of all problems to bring to task? For the past several months I had invested hours of research, studying the tragic and tear-jerking stories and the psychological implications of sex trafficking. The crime is now bigger than drugs, and the worst part? The public is unaware. I studied all the ugly details, how they lure twelve-year-old girls into their stables and the horrifying ways they keep them from running away. And the most terrifying fact of all? The market for sex is huge. That is the real crime. Our society, our culture looks the other way, pretending it doesn't exist, yet it grows larger every year.

The picture is as glamorous as a garbage dump. And when the girls are used up? Like my granddaughter, my dear Jasmine, they are cast off and left to die.

"Would you like me to go with you? We could go up in the motorhome."

"Yes. I would, but I'm flying out this morning. Brent is taking me to the airport now."

"I'll drive up. I'll leave this afternoon and be there tomorrow. You can stay with me in the motorhome."

"Okay. Thanks, Mom."

Thanks Mom. Those two words sent my emotions roiling like the ocean's waves in a hurricane. I heard the fifteen years of hurt and pain and guilt in Charlotte's voice, the torture she suffered as the result of her daughter's lifestyle. As a mother I knew her pain. But now, I can be supportive. Something I had never been capable of offering her before. I recalled a friend's words who had counseled me during those heartbreaking times with my daughter, when I didn't want to live because I had felt like a failure to Charlotte. I had cried to my friend, telling her how much I was hurting. My friend's response? "Good," she said. "Someday you will be able to share with someone else who is going through the same thing, how you got through it."

I would be there for Jasmine, too. I wondered if she would remember me.

I would have thought my granddaughter was anorexic if I had seen her on the street.

Charlotte greeted her daughter with forced cheer, her voice tight and high-pitched. "Hi Jasmine. How are you doing?"

I cringed at the scene before me. Jasmine's thinness shouted at me, but the girl answered her mother only in a whispered mumble, which came out as a moan, too weak to form the words. Her dry lips, shiny with glittering lip balm, did not move. Her neon-pink fingernails tapped mindlessly against the lip balm applicator clutched in her frail fingers.

"Do you remember your Grandma Janice?" After kissing her daughter, Charlotte stood at the foot of the bed, watching Jasmine intently. Jasmine turned her head only enough to look at me. She moaned again.

"Oh hi." I felt as if a light in her soul flickered slightly brighter.

But it might have been my wishful thinking.

Charlotte and I spent four days camped in the Walmart parking lot across the street from the hospital. I was able to catch some time alone with Jasmine and we talked about her experiences in "The Life." She told me of the uglies and the dangers which no one needed to hear except a grandmother who understood without judgement. Jasmine admitted to me she would return to 'The Life" if she recovered. And yet, when I asked her, "If you had a sixteen-year-old daughter, would you want her to go back?" Her answer? A definite, "No."

Back in the motorhome in the evenings, Charlotte and I watched TV and shared only small talk to avoid discussing the dire condition of Jasmine. When the surgery was completed and Jasmine stable, Charlotte arranged for her baby girl to be transported to a hospital closer to home. We told Jasmine good-bye and we would see her soon. We didn't cry, nor did Jasmine, but the sorrow was thick.

After a short stay at the Redlands Community Hospital, when all that could be done was done, Jasmine finally came home … and hospice care was arranged. Jasmine hung on to spend her last Christmas with her son and family.

Jasmine was twenty-eight when she passed. She left behind a delightful eight-year-old son.

CHAPTER FORTY-TWO
2016

By the time the New Year rolled around, my relationship with Charlotte had deepened, our trust in one another had grown stronger, and we began to settle into our new roles. I readied my motorhome to head out on book tours, as I did every year. The tour would take me across the country, signing books, fulfilling speaking engagements and presenting writing seminars.

My first day back on the road, I leaned back in the driver's seat. I didn't feel so alone. I felt Maggie's spirit traveling with me as my Nate had done after he passed away. Fueled by the hypnotic drone of the tires and the sway of the motorhome, my thoughts and dreams began to soar, opening up my mind and easing the grief I had carried the last six months.

Through my motor home windshield, the world spread out before me. The wide-open expanse of the desert fed my thirsty spirit like a lost traveler in search of water. I wanted to swoon and cry from the promise and the joy of the freedoms awaiting me. Amping up the volume on my playlist, George Strait's silky drawl filled the cab *"There's a difference between living and living well." "You can't have it all, all by yourself…"*

Perhaps the song struck a chord, or perhaps I was still reeling from the nostalgia of my first holiday season with Charlotte and my grandchildren and great grandchildren. Everyone had brought their special Thanksgiving dishes and Christmas sides. Food — The antidote for strained relationships, providing a healing balm for everyone to bond and enjoy the special days and friendly banter.

Comfortable with her family and having many holiday seasons under her belt, no matter how many butterflies she felt, Charlotte had pulled off this holiday as routine. But for me, the family, the Thanksgiving dinner, the Christmas presents, the children's' excitement on Christmas morning — all of it, were far from ordinary. Instead, those days became the happy ending in a novel, the magical climax of a fantasy storybook, all the result of Margaret's Grieving Gift, which just seemed to keep on giving. I attempted to hold each moment close, trying to revere every one.

I shrugged, shaking off the discontentment the country song stirred in me. Rolling my eyes up at the puffy white clouds which shadowed the desert floor, I thought, *"Really? After all you have received? That's not enough?"*

The Grieving Gift had not been a soul mate. The idea had only been a silly suggestion to make Maggie laugh. Geez! How could I be so crazy-greedy to want more? I was on my own for finding a soul mate.

So, it's true. On a death watch, you do get to know someone. I discovered more than I cared to know about my sister. Yet in the end, I also discovered her love for me on a deeper level than I ever imagined. When she called me Turn, when she squeezed my hand, and the day she clapped, all moments which assured me we weren't just sisters. We were each a part of a whole. When she died, a part of me died, too. So, she didn't make her last journey alone. But the good side is part of her now lives on within me. She is here when I hear a particular song that she liked, when I visit a beautiful garden, and when I pick berries from the vine.

I breathed the sage scented air deep into my lungs. Maggie's Grieving Gift gave me a certainty that she had found her way and was at peace. Like I had told her, you are not "just dead" when you die. I'll bet she was surprised.

After a cold dry night, the Arizona's March sun had a habit of greeting the day in a welcoming way. The Tucson fiery globe warmed the musky earth, still damp from the monsoons. Its rays reflected off the craggy mountainous backdrop. As was its tendency, El Sol produced a majestic gala in the heavens, deceiving the awestruck Arizona tourist, who is unfamiliar with the fact that this is the same fiery ball, which in the summer, blisters everything to a meaty crisp, like a burnt burger left on the grill too long.

Settling into the campsite, I kicked the chaise lounge back so I could gaze up at the cloudless sky. Beside me, Marmalade stretched out on the still cool grass.

Yesterday I presented the last writing seminar of my series to an RV rally here at the fairgrounds. Relaxing, I cupped both hands around my coffee mug and rested it on my bended knees. I looked forward to a week's break before a book signing at the Tucson Festival of Books at the University of Arizona. The coming week would give me time to scratch off the many items on my marketing To-Do list.

I absorbed the spectacular sunrise while my thumb counted on my fingers, October, November .... and March. I struggled to sort out the meanings of the whirlwind of events which had occurred during the last six months. For eight years, since my sister's diagnosis, I shuddered at the thought facing a bleak, lonely future without her. I anticipated my loss to be intense. I couldn't count how many times I asked myself, "Who's going to have your back now?"

The answer was always, "There will be no one for me."

And now? Look at me. I scoffed at the fears that never came to pass. No one can predict the future.

The sunrise stroked the landscape, painting the endless vista into a red and golden magnificence. Margaret had rode with me several times and had sat beside me, sharing peaceful views like this. My heart twisted, ready to react to the memory, but then, just as quickly, the faces of Charlotte and her beautiful family appeared in my mind's eye.

"I know this was your doing, Margaret," I said aloud.

Marmalade's ears swiveled back in my direction. I grinned at him. "You know don't you, Marmalade? Cat's know these kinds of things," I said.

He chirped, but didn't turn his head. Instead, he focused on a leaf skittering across the campsite, chased by the morning breeze.

As I posted photos to Facebook of yesterday's horse show which had taken place here at the fairgrounds, the familiar notification ping sounded on my phone.

"Beautiful horses! Do you ride?" A Facebook friend asked.

"Not anymore," I answered. *"But in high school my best girlfriend and I rode all the time. Every weekend we rode from daylight to dusk. Our parents didn't care where we went. The only rule was, 'Be home by dark'. Those poor horses were dragging their hooves by the end of the weekend."*

I drifted into the memories with my best friend, Barbara, a time when I was pure and the world was a wonderment waiting to be explored. *"It was the best time of my life."*

On a whim I googled Barbara's name. When it popped up on LinkedIn I stared at her name. She lived in Tucson!

Without thinking, I tapped in her number. As the cell rang, possibilities jumped into my mind. Would she hang up when she found out it was me? What happened all those years ago? She picked up on the second ring before I could talk myself into hanging up. My throat tightened when she said hello.

"Barbara? This is Janice Harvey… from Springfield High School." She didn't respond. It was too late to hang up. "Your friend from Springfield High?"

A longer pause. And then, "Oh my! Janice Harvey! Is that you? Oh my!"

I released the breath I had been holding. I told her my long-convoluted story about posting the horse show photos on Facebook and a friend asking if I ride and how I think of our times together whenever I see horses. "I'm here in Tucson to attend the book festival. Do you want to meet and catch up?"

"Oh my, goodness! Yes! It's so great to talk to you! I've written a book, too! I'll be at the book festival, too! My, it's such a small world."

Her laughter reminded me of the bell that rang every time an angel got its wings in the movie, *It's A Wonderful Life.*

"Of course we have to get together!" She said. "My business is designing wedding invitations. I'm finishing up a big wedding order before the festival. How about we meet up afterward, on Sunday and talk old times?" Her voice sang with a tone of mischievousness just as it had in high school when we plunged our horses into a pond that we shouldn't ha or when we talked about boys.

"Where are you staying? I'll pick you up. We'll go to dinner."

CHAPTER FORTY-THREE
2016

Our conversation on the ride to the restaurant reminded me of the huge flock of birds who gathered every evening in a tree in front of my house, chirping and sharing whatever birds have to say to one another. The cacophony continued non-stop until the sun went down.

Our chatter filled the car like that tree full of birds at home. We shared the highlights of our last fifty years. She was divorced, two children and more grandchildren. She had lived in Tucson thirty years, running a wedding invitation business. The book she'd written? No surprise. About horses.

At dinner, we laughed and talked non-stop, grabbing only quick bites as our food turned cold. It was as if no time had passed. The years had not stolen her innocence and gaiety. She brought up all the many fun, and often times dangerous, escapades we experienced, where up until now, I had only recalled my painful times.

"I attended the 50th Reunion," Barbara said.

"I wanted to attend, but my sister was very ill. I couldn't make it."

"Do you remember Betty Conner?" I shook my head. "How about Chet Rivers? Or Bobby Wheaton?"

I shook my head at each name. "I don't remember anyone," I said.

"I'm on the Springfield High School Facebook page," she said. "Are you?"

"No. I never joined. I figured why should I? I couldn't remember anyone. To be exact, I remember only three people." I held up three fingers and pulled back the first digit. "I remember you." I pulled back the second digit. "I remember Tamara. Was she at the reunion?"

"Tamara passed away last year."

"Oh, no," I said. "It doesn't seem right, her not being here with us, does it?"

Barb shook her head. We paused, lost in our memories. I shook off the sadness and pulled down my third remaining finger. "And I remember Gary Smith. Do you remember him?"

In a sultry voice, Barb grinned. "Oh, yes. Everyone remembers Gary."

"Did you see him at the reunion?"

My pulse quickened as I awaited her answer. Swallowing hard, I exhaled a deep breath, which I hadn't realized I'd been holding. I might have blushed. My face felt hot from the embarrassment of my body's reaction. I worried Barbara might notice.

"I don't know," she answered. "I didn't see him. Maybe he's dead."

My spirit withered like a pricked bright yellow balloon. I leaned back in the restaurant booth.

"Of course," I finally said. "I forget that we're all almost seventy." I dusted some crumbs off the table and lined up my silverware.

Barbara brought out the yearbooks she'd brought, and with her prodding, I remembered Kathy, the girl in the bathroom on my first day returning to school who had greeted me so kindly.

"Welcome back," she had said. Just two words, but I never forgot them. They had meant everything to me. Barbara gave me Kathy's contact information. I wanted her to know what a difference she had made that day.

At that particular moment the thought struck me, Kathy and Gary were the only two people who had not treated me as if I were invisible. Both of them had made all the difference in the world to me.

Barbara plopped back against the back of restaurant booth, laughing. "This is so fun! I am so glad you called. "Are you still grooming dogs? I remember your little shop in your parents' basement. You taught me how to groom my little poodle." She shook her head. "You've brought back so many memories."

"I sold my grooming business last year. I am an author now, I write full time. Right now I'm busy finishing up the last chapters of two books."

"You stay busy like me. I'm pushing to get my house paid off by next year. Then I want to travel." Her voice still sang with a mischievous tilt. "Who knows, maybe I'll get something small, like one of those little tear drop trailers, and tag along with you."

"Wouldn't that be fun? I'm going to travel Route 66 all the way back to Springfield. "I promised my sister I would go to all our haunts and think of her. " I want to visit all the places we used to go, like the lake where we ice skated, and the grove where we went walnut hunting, and where we floated on inner tubes on the Sangamon River. You can follow along in your little trailer. I can see it now. It would be hot pink."

A shadow clouded Barbara's expression, darkening her devil may care attitude. "We'll see," she said. "My goal right now is to be debt free by next year. But who knows! I might just do that!"

"I'm not heading out until August. So, you have four months to buy that little Casita and pack it up."

"Oh, Janice you're such a free spirit."

I saw the longing in her eyes. "I'll visit all our hangouts, too. You know, like Bob's Big Boy and

McDonald's? And all the places we went riding, too, like Washington Park."

Barbara shook her head. "The stables are no longer there. It's all houses now."

"I'm sure everything has changed. The last time I visited Springfield was in 1987 when my sister and I attended an aunt's 50th wedding anniversary.

I told Barbara how Gary visited me at the hotel, and how I tried to look him up after my Nate died. "I was going to try to find him when I went back in August. But, if he's passed….."

My voice trailed off. When I noticed Barbara staring at me, I sat up. Shoving my whimsical fantasies back in their fifty-year-old box, I laid my napkin on the table and said, 'I'd better get going." I checked my watch. "Wow! I can't believe the time. They're going to kick us out of here."

After Barb and I parted, promising to keep in touch, I returned to my rig and stretched out while the television droned in the background.

Barbara and I had picked up right where we left off fifty years ago. I asked her if she had known about my pregnancy.

"I didn't know what had happened to you," she had answered. "You just disappeared."

I wondered if she told the truth. But even if she had known, her parents would not have not allowed the relationship to continue. Society had labeled me a slut. Times were different. I smirked. Today, it was more common to be pregnant in high school than not.

Driving back to California the next morning, I listened to the soothing hum of the motorhome tires and basked in the warmth of a second reunion within six months of my Maggie's passing. My big sister was really out-doing herself with this Grieving Gift thing.

If Barbara's information was correct I guessed that any reunions with Gary would not take place between the sheets, but only between the pages of my books where he already lived in four of them.

I read somewhere if an author loves you, you will live forever.

CHAPTER FORTY- FOUR
2016

Every time I returned from a trip, once I turned the corner and could see that my house still stood at the end of the street, I always gave a small sigh of relief. I guess we all worry that our stuff will be safe while we are gone. I pulled into my drive, shut off the engine and hit the remote. The garage door crept up. Home sweet home. All my things remained where I left them. A month's worth of mail spilled out onto the garage floor from the mail slot. I would spend the next hour or two unloading the motorhome of food and clothes and then sorting through a pound or two of junk mail.

But Marmalade goes in first. He, too, always knew we were home when we rounded the corner. He wiggled, like he always does, demanding to be released from my arms, into the laundry room where his food and water dishes were. He, too, worried about his stuff. He sniffed his dishes thoroughly and meowed in satisfaction, relieved, I guessed like me, that everything remained the same as when he had left.

I started a load in the washer and then walked the property's perimeter picking at a few weeds or piece of trash which had blown into my rock yard. Later in the evening, I would hose off a month's worth of accumulated dust and leaves from the back patio and the walkway that led to the front door. As I watered the plants, decorating the walkway to the front door, neighbors called out on their evening walks, "Welcome home." "Missed you." "Glad you're back, hope you had a great time." Coming home to neighbors and friends whom I had known for years offered up a good feeling of belonging to the community. Inside, the furniture had gathered its own layer of dust, too, but dusting and vacuuming could wait until tomorrow, along with washing the road dirt from the car and the motorhome.

So much to do when you own a house. For the last several years, the tasks of loading and unloading the motorhome , of catching up on household chores when I returned and the continuing upkeep of both the house and the motorhome became more and more tiresome.

I toyed with the idea of renting the house out and living full time in my motorhome. My life would be traveling and writing, my two passions fulfilled. Since my sister passed, the urge had grown stronger. I considered Charlotte and the grandchildren and their busy lives. I would still take advantage of the good weather of California winters in order to share the holidays with them.

But for now, I finished my chores, took a long, hot shower, enjoying the huge bathroom, and relaxed in front of my big screen TV. It had been a long day.

I caught up with several of my recorded shows before my eyes became like heavy weights. Turning off the TV and the lights, I padded down the hall, eager to sink into my queen sized bed.

The California night breeze drifted into the room like a sweet surprise, chasing away the month of staleness. A contentedness flowed in my veins, giving me a rush like the tingle of good sex. It couldn't get much better than this. Once again, I reviewed the past and where I had come from. The ugliness I had lived had, not only been forgiven, but replaced with a promising future that I could never have imagined, a future full of caring, loving people, whom I had never even dared to hope for. If this was as good as it gets, I had no complaints.

Oh, but I had dreamed of more. I had never been able to control my dreams.

The familiar ding from Facebook messenger cut into my musings, invading my bedroom like an interloper.

"You have a friend request from Gary Smith."
I sprang up from the bed. My heart raced like nothing I had ever experienced. I thought my chest might explode. For a milli-second I made a feeble attempt to grasp what was happening to me. I couldn't. I didn't care. I had no control. My head was spinning. My heart, in charge now, demanded to have what it had lost fifty years ago. I pounded the "accept" button so hard the phone fell from my grip.
Picking it up, it dinged again.
"Hello, old friend."

The End

ABOUT THE AUTHOR
JUDY HOWARD

Judy Howard's mailing address is San Bernardino, California, but you will rarely find her there. Instead, check out the Auto Club Motor Speedway in Fontana, California. Raise the visor on the driver's Mario Andretti racing helmet. You might find her. Judy Howard, one of the top ranking Amazon authors, might be strapped in and ready to race.

Or cruise down Route 66. Keep your eyes open for her Winnebago motorhome which she's named, "The Big Story," which tows behind it her Smart Car she calls "The Short Story."

You might have caught sight of her on the unpopulated beaches of Oregon, or visiting the raging Niagara Falls, or rafting in the Grand Canyon.

Of one thing, you can be sure, she's a thrill seeker, a firecracker and a lover of an amazing sunset. Judy Howard and her cat, Sportster, do not stay in one place for long. But first, she is a writer.

The genre of her books are as varied as the places she chooses to park her motorhome. She has written a memoir, a thriller-romance, a reality fiction, and an autobiographical novel.

Her cat, Sportster, too, has pounced into the writing game with his own book for young adults, ACTIVATE LION MODE.

But all of Howard's and Sportster's books carry the same theme --overcoming life's difficulties.

Judy Howard travels across the United States as a motivational speaker and a presenter of writing seminars. When asked, "Why do you write?" Howard answers —

"As Authors we can change the world. Our voices can make a difference. I hope to inspire others to find their quiet voice inside that tells them to take the dare, to live that life which, until now, they have only dreamed."

Website: Judy Howard Publishing

Jhoward1935@gmail.com

Coming Soon

TRUCK STOP
By
Judy Howard

CHAPTER ONE

The trailer park slept, its occupants buried deep in their unfulfilled dreams. The Triumph's glass pipes rumbled soft against the aluminum siding of the Spartan trailer. Inside, the front curtain on the wrap around window parted slightly. Outside, the biker waited as a worn out Honda Civic sputtered down the row of mobile homes and pulled out onto the road. Like a full moon on Christmas Eve, the street lamps lit up the trail of ghost-blue fog of exhaust that hung low on the asphalt. The biker hit the kill switch and quiet returned to the mobile home community. He swung his lanky leg over the bike and dismounted.

Moving slowly, not with uncertainty, but more with restrained anticipation, he yanked off his fingerless gloves and unsnapped the helmet's chinstrap. The click of the snap, the squeak of his leather jacket and crunch of his boots on the gravel overrode the silent pounding in his chest. He threw his gloves inside the helmet and ran his fingers through his hair. The curtain fell back in place as he strode up the stepping-stones to the trailer's door. Raising his fist to knock, the door swung open.

She stood in her baby dolls. A flicker of candlelight danced across her exposed midriff. Stiff legged, in a wide stance he stared. She giggled. The ninety miles he traveled to see her, always gave him time to think. It was not the first time he made the ride and probably would not be the last. He had been younger the first time and he had never had a lover. He was eighteen now, not old enough yet to be feeling the buzz from the beer burning in his veins, but he didn't care. He didn't care about anything but the night's promise standing before him.

Budding with the power she knew she possessed, she swung the door open wider. The heat from the trailer touched his face like a feather. He thought of his sophomore and junior years, watching her moving through the halls from class to class. Her gaze always met his as he passed, then quickly dropped to stare at the floor. Now, she held him with those passionate baby blues, leaving him weak with anticipation.

"Are you coming inside? She shivered. "It's cold."

He shoved his shaking hands into his pockets and stepped inside.

www.JudyHowardPublishing.com

jhoward1935@gmail.com

Also Coming soon!

ACTIVATE LOVE MODE
By
~~Judy Howard~~
Sportster The Cat

CHAPTER ONE

"**F**or he's a jolly good cat! For he's a jolly good cat!"
    The campfire farewell party kept me up past my bedtime.
The rangers and staff at Yellowstone National Park, along with many campers, whom I had met over the past weeks huddled in a semicircle, chanting the offbeat, off key song. Hunching over steaming cups

of coffee and cocoa, their faces glowed and flickered from the reflections of the campfire.

Judy, leaned back in her chair, stretched out her legs and crossed them at her ankles. She cupped her hands around the warm mug of tea and smiled down at me.

I bellowed out a loud meow, jumped into my director's chair and snuggled into my lap blanket. The fleecy throw, imprinted with the National Park Service's logo and the image of Yellowstone's "Old Faithful" geyser and had been a gift from Ranger Dave, the NPS communications director, who hired me as an ambassador, a new concept for a the NPS. My duties, much like that of Smokey the Bear, were to preserve and protect our forests and bring good will. Printed on the back of my director's chair, also a gift from the park service, was *Sportster, Ambassador to the Friends of The Forest*.

Joan, the campground host, a gentle soul, kind of thick at her waist wore a period sun bonnet over greying hair pulled back into a bun. Standing beside Judy and me, she led the crowd, as they all belted out the last verse of *For He's A Jolly Good Fellow*. ".......which nobody can deny!"

Everyone raised their mugs in my direction. "Here! Here! Yeah Sportster!"

Ranger Dave, the NPS communications director, broke from the circle and approached Judy and me. He leaned down and scratched my ears. "For a small cat you've certainly made a big impression on these folks, Sportster. You are one special cat."

I hoped he wasn't going to try to pick me up. I hate that. But he held back, and only petted me on the head. I returned the favor and rubbed up against his hand.

Straightening, he stood next to Joan and turned and faced the crowd. "Thank you all for giving Sportster and Judy such a great send off. I hope you all have enjoyed their nature walks."

I know I did. Judy and I explored many of the trails. While Judy talked about the fauna and creatures, I pointed out the exciting scents on every leaf, pine needle and stick along the way.

"Many of you have asked how Sportster came upon his position as ambassador for NPS." He glanced down at me with a big smile. "Sportster drew my attention when I came across his heroic story on the internet. He and Judy were a part of a breaking story in which this little guy became involved in rescuing a twelve year old girl, who had been kidnapped by a major human trafficking ring in Portland, Oregon.

"His story went viral.

"At the time the National Park Service was looking for a fresh face for their marketing campaign and this little guy fit our image, appealing and charming —in our words — and distinguished and daring, I'm sure, in Sportster's words. If he could speak for himself."

Why does everyone refer to me as 'Little Guy'? I switched my tail and shifted around in the camp chair.

"Anyway," Ranger Dave continued, "that's a story for another campfire." He turned and addressed Joan. "Joan, I understand you have a special treat for Sportster tonight that the children have made."

Joan and her cat, Rumpa, short for Rumpelstiltskin, took morning walks with Judy and me every day.

"Yes We I do." Joan leaned down and offered me a treat. I took it, crunch it down and looked for more. She scratched my chin and then pulled an object out from under her other arm. I sniffed her fingers for a couple more pieces of kibble, tuna flavored, my favorite but she faced the children gathered around the campfire.

"Kids what does our friend Joan have tucked under her arm? Do you know?" Ranger Dave scanned the group with a mischievous smile.

A couple youngsters jumped up, bursting with excitement. "Yes! A present for Ambassador Sportster!"

"Yes it is," Ranger Dave said. "A gift for his dedication to help preserve our forests and wildlife." Ranger Dave chuckled and the children tittered.

Joan held up a handmade plaque which the children had created in their craft workshop. "Ambassador Sportster, we all are excited about the work you're doing for the National Park Service," Joan said. "For that reason we are proud to present you with this plaque to honor the work you are doing to educate, protect and preserve our national parks."

"Yeah! Sportster!!

The applause and admiration flustered me. The praise seemed a little over the top for a cat who came from the streets, but I sat a little taller and sniffed the construction paper covered with photos, pine cones and sticks and leaves, held together with Elmer 's glue. I like to lick glue.

Giggling the children jumped up and down, proud of their piece of art.

When I was a young tomcat I did not have the life like these children enjoyed, I grew up alone and homeless on some bad streets of Sun City, California.. I never knew what threat waited for me around the next corner.

I didn't know who my father was. Mom told me one day he yelled out a loud caterwaul, leaped back over the fence from where he had come, and disappeared, leaving my mom with nothing left but his memory, me and six siblings.

I remember the story well, as she licked my face clean and nudged me close to her.

I dreamed of him and couldn't understand why he left us, but I understood the hardship Mom suffered feeding us. I watched it take its toll on her as she grew bone thin. Hunting all night, Many times she crept home after hunting all night. She bore wounds from fighting over a prize morsel of food found in a sooty gutter. Listening to the mews and meows from my siblings, I could no longer endure the sadness and desperation.

Still very young, and always hungry, I refused my meager share Mom offered. I was only a burden. I struck out on my own.

My hunting prowess lacked experience. Weeks passed. I wrestled with the idea of going back. When the loneliness and hunger became unbearable I abandoned my convictions and returned to the den. Only a faint scent remained. I sniffed the cold ground that had always been warmed by my siblings. My family had disappeared I circled the area rooting and pawing to find a dropped morsel of food. A tuft of mom's hair which had snagged on the branch of the bush, loosened and whirled into the air, the final piece of my former life disappeared.

www.JudyHowardPublishing.com
jhoward1935@gmail.com